KURT KAMM

THE LIZARD'S TALE

Published by MCM Publishing, a division of Monkey C Media
mcmpublishing.com
Book Design by Monkey C Media
monkeycmedia.com

Edited by Jennifer Silva Redmond

Printed in the United States of America

Publisher's Cataloging in Publication Data

Names: Kamm, Kurt L., author.
Title: The Lizard's Tale / Kurt Kamm.
Description: San Diego : MCM Publishing, 2016.
Identifiers: ISBN: 978-0-9974413-0-7
Subjects: LCSH: Drug traffic--Mexico--Fiction. | Drug traffic--California-
                -Prevention--Fiction. | Drug dealers--Mexico--Fiction. |
                Organized crime--Mexico--Fiction. | Drug enforcement agents
                --United States--Fiction. | Game wardens--California--Santa
                Catalina Island--Fiction. | LCGFT: Detective and mystery
                fiction. | Thrillers (Fiction) | BISAC: FICTION / Thrillers /
                Suspense. | FICTION / Mystery & Detective / International
                Mystery & Crime. | FICTION / Thrillers / Crime.
Classification: LCC: PS3611.A4686 L59 2016 | DDC: 813/.6--dc23

For Denise Middlebrooks

CONTENTS

I   Alejandro 7

II   The Lizard 46

III   The Cuiza 48

IV   The Lizard............................. 94

V   Ryan 97

VI   The Lizard 134

VII   Gina 136

VIII The Lizard 186

IX   Jose Miguel 188

Acknowledgments 202

About the Author 203

1 | ALEJANDRO

Alejandro Luna waited for weeks. He grew impatient, then anxious, and finally sank into dejection. He gave up hope, concluding it wasn't going to happen—it couldn't be done. He walked around his house in a black mood. Days passed and he barely spoke to his wife.

Finally, Jose Miguel called late on a Sunday evening. "Yes," he told Alejandro. "I have it. Come now."

Alejandro was angry. "What took so long?" he asked. It was already the third week of April, almost the end of the dry season.

Guatemala has only two seasons—dry and wet. Soon the torrential rains would come, triggering massive mudslides, and washing away roads. The downpours would turn the *terracería*—the unpaved roads through the jungle and mountains—into a sea of mud, making his journey all the more dangerous.

After his conversation with Jose Miguel, Alejandro told his wife he was leaving early the next morning.

"Where are you going?" she asked. "How long will you be away?"

"The Rainforest Alliance is meeting with the coffee farmers in Huehuetenango," he said. "They're introducing a program for sustainable farming and the Ministry has asked me to attend." Alejandro searched her face for signs of disbelief, but saw none. "I'll be back in less than a week if the weather is dry, ten days at the most." The weather was only one of his worries, but he didn't elaborate.

"What about the environmental conference?"

"It's not until next month."

"I hate it when you're away. I hope someday you'll have a job that lets you stay at home."

"Someday," he said, and kissed her. "When I come back, we'll go out for a good dinner."

Alejandro spent the evening making his final preparations. The General—an old Land Cruiser—was waiting and ready to go. A general in the Guatemalan army had driven it, and when he tired of it, he passed it on to the Ministry of the Interior. Eventually Alejandro's boss at the Ministry allowed him to use it for work. Alejandro had spent his own precious savings to prepare the General for the trip. He had replaced the tires, tuned the engine, and repaired the transmission so that for the first time in ten years, the four-wheel drive functioned. The air-conditioning barely worked, but that didn't matter. It was good enough to keep the inside of the vehicle around 25 degrees Celsius and Alejandro could live with that. If he had to drive up the Pacific Coast of Mexico bathed in sweat, he would do it.

He placed a small bag with clean clothes—shorts, pants, and several shirts—behind the front seat of the Land Cruiser. He took his father's old Colt .45 from the top shelf of his closet. He cleaned and oiled it, made sure it had a full clip, and locked it in the steel box welded to the underside of the driver's seat. He tied two full plastic gas containers to the roof rack, and made sure his machete was in the back along with the shovel he carried for emergencies.

After a short night of fitful sleep, Alejandro arose before dawn, full of nervous energy. He dressed quickly, splashed water on his face, and washed down mouthfuls of black beans and chorizo with two cups of bitter coffee. He had to take food—he certainly wouldn't find a *mercado* in the jungle, where the people survived on subsistence farming, so he packed a cooler with potato tamales wrapped in cornhusks, fried pork, strips of *carne seca*, plantains, and his favorite breakfast bread, *pan dulce*. He added several bottles of water and took a dozen Coca-Colas for extra caffeine. He also included three bottles of Cerveza Gallo, his favorite beer, for brief celebrations at milestones along his journey. Alejandro poured his remaining coffee into an old thermos and was on his way out the door when he remembered the most important thing—the paper bag containing half a dozen small, brown birds' eggs. The bird's eggs! How could he forget them?

His wife was still asleep when he left his *casita* on the north side of Guatemala City. The first rays of sun had not yet lit the sky and it was still relatively cool, around 20 degrees Celsius. By mid-day the temperature would climb another twelve degrees and then he would be driving in the heat. Alejandro knew CA9, the Ruta al Atlantico, like the palm of his hand. The first thirty kilometers from Guatemala City offered two well-paved lanes in each direction, and that would be the easiest part of his entire trip. Farther on, still travelling northeast, he would cover another 120 kilometers on a crowded, two-lane highway where the only speed limit was how fast you chose to drive. He was headed into the rural lowlands of the Motagua River Valley, near the border with Honduras.

In that near-desert area—one of the driest in Central America—Jose Miguel was waiting for him, in the tiny village of Estanzuela. On another day, Alejandro might have planned to stop to purchase some of the region's hand-rolled cigars crafted from local tobacco, but this was not a pleasure trip and there was no time to be wasted. By noon, he wanted to be back on the road headed west toward the Mexican border.

He had travelled less than five kilometers, listening to the hum of his new tires on the pavement, when the traffic slowed to a crawl and then stopped altogether. Alejandro sat in the early light of dawn, drummed his fingers on the steering wheel, and waited for the traffic to clear. To pass the time, he thought about the money. How would it feel in his hands? American money was crisp and clean, and so much more valuable than the Guatemalan Quetzal.

He turned off the engine to save gas and watched with mounting frustration as scooters and motorcycles passed by, winding through the sea of immobile vehicles. Forty minutes later—it seemed like hours—the traffic began to crawl forward. In the growing light, Alejandro saw the problem up ahead. Automobiles, buses, and trucks were squeezing into one lane and then slowly moving off the highway to pass an accident. A camioneta, one of the colorful recycled American school buses everyone referred to as a chicken bus, had collided with a livestock truck travelling the opposite direction. The *camioneta* lay on its side, blocking both the eastbound lanes. Baskets of produce, suitcases, and cardboard cartons that had been tied to the roof were scattered across the highway. As he crept past, Alejandro saw several injured bus passengers sitting on the pavement. The truck, stopped in the middle of an oncoming lane, was still upright, but its front end had been badly damaged. The driver paced around at the side of the road, talking on a cell phone. As Alejandro passed the truck, he saw several dead goats lying on the road, their blood seeping across the asphalt. There was no sign of anyone from the National Police Traffic Division, but that was no surprise. The officers didn't come on duty until 6:00 a.m.—if they came to work at all.

Alejandro bounced in his seat as the General climbed back onto the highway. This was a bad omen in the first minutes of a long journey, and he sent a quick prayer to Saint Christopher.

He drove into the morning sun, paralleling the course of the Rio Motagua, Guatemala's longest river, which crossed from west to east and eventually flowed into the Caribbean Ocean. Alejandro travelled through the cactus-dotted semi-arid Guatemalan flatlands, the blue-green outlines of the Sierra de Las Minas in the distance off to his left. Thousands of years of jungle growth had created cloud forests on the sides of these mountains, some of which were extinct volcanos 3,000 meters high. He was more than an hour behind schedule because of the accident, and drove as fast as possible through the dry, unforgiving landscape of the Motagua River Valley. It was almost noon before he reached Estanzuela, a small town of 11,000, nestled in one of the depressions formed by the Motagua, a river polluted with untreated sewage and garbage from Guatemala City.

Alejandro was an *ingeniero agrónomo*—an agricultural engineer—and travelled throughout Guatemala trying to help farmers break their cycle of subsistence agriculture and rise above their poverty. He worked the small agricultural towns, bringing hybrid seed from the Ministry of the Interior, and tried to teach the native farmers better skills to increase their crop yields. Some listened, some didn't. Many spoke only their local dialect and barely understood what he was telling them.

His country was poor and backward. Twenty years after a long and devastating civil war, it was still a struggling third-world nation with the highest rate of malnutrition in the Western Hemisphere.

Decades ago, his father had been an unimportant journalist who made the mistake of writing something critical of the ruling military junta. One day in 1983, when Alejandro was 15, his father didn't come home, and eventually his name was added to the list of 50,000 other *desapariciones forzadas*—forced disappearances—carried out by shadowy military groups. Alejandro was bright and literate, and managed to survive the loss of his father. He studied hard, attended the Central National School of Agriculture, and was lucky enough to find a job with the Ministry of the Interior. When he began work, he had dreams of better things to come—for his country and for himself. Unfortunately, life had only gotten worse and he'd watched Guatemala sink into a pit of corruption and narco-crime. The politicians, the police, even the army—all were dishonest. His boss at the Ministry of the Interior was corrupt, and his boss's boss was corrupt. If they weren't stealing public funds, they were involved with the Mexican drug cartels. At forty-seven, Alejandro was disillusioned and angry, and had decided it was time to take something for himself and his wife.

He turned off the highway onto the narrow cobblestone streets of Estanzuela, passing a small stand where two old women sold the decorative white peasant blouses and colorful cloth woven by the locals. When he reached the *central,* he saw Jose Miguel's truck parked on the far side.

Jose Miguel was a big man with a belly that hung over his belt. He stood by his battered truck and watched the Land Cruiser approach. He wore a straw hat, but the sun was hot, and sweat ran down his cheeks. Nearby, a woman was selling sizzling tortillas and fresh tropical fruits. Jose Miguel inhaled the aroma of the tortillas and his mouth watered. He had expected the *ingeniero* over an hour ago. He was hungry, but couldn't leave the valuable cargo unguarded. He wanted to transfer the cargo to the Land Cruiser as fast as possible and be finished with this business.

Jose Miguel had his doubts about what they were doing. He knew it was wrong, but he wanted the money—no, he *needed* the money. His first responsibility was to his wife and to his son Ricardo, named for Guatemala's most popular singer, Ricardo Arjona. Jose Miguel had hoped his son would be as handsome as the great singer, but the boy had been born with a hideous harelip which only surgery could fix. Jose

Miguel was a poor man who struggled to feed his wife and son, and the money from the transaction was the only way he could pay the Hospital de la Familia to repair the ugly gash in the middle of Ricardo's face.

He walked to the back of his truck, lifted the canvas and glanced underneath. Then he looked across the plaza where the City Hall and the police headquarters were clustered together. What if one of the officers from the National Civil Police decided at this very moment to walk across the park and inspect his truck? What if he looked under the canvas? Hah! What if the sun failed to rise in the morning? The fat police were too busy eating tamales and planning their next drug deal. Jose Miguel tugged the canvas back in place and got behind the wheel.

"I want to be paid up front," he had told the *ingeniero* when they first discussed the transaction. "I want my money now." Could he trust the *ingeniero*? He had worked for this man from the Ministry off and on for five years, helping him get to some of the remote farms and plantations in the eastern lowlands and communicate with the people, but how well did he really know him? Jose Miguel had never done anything like this. Would he be paid? If not, what could he do about it?

"It's not possible to pay you now," the *ingeniero* had said. "I don't have the money." He had pulled some bills out of his pocket and counted them. "All I can give you now is 240 Quetzals, that's what I have." He had waved the money in front of Jose Miguel. "You can take this, or wait until I get paid. Then I'll come back and give you your share. Four hundred American dollars. Think about that. Four one-hundred Yankee dollar bills."

Jose Miguel did think about it. He had never actually seen any American money. Four-hundred dollars was an incredible fortune—more than enough to pay for Ricardo's operation. He might even have something left over to repair his truck. Jose Miguel had agreed, but later, after that discussion months ago, he had decided $400 was not enough.

After all, this was a dangerous transaction and he began to worry that the *ingeniero* was cheating him. He was entitled to more. Much more. He decided to ask for $500.

"*Puchica!*" the *ingeniero* had exclaimed when Jose Miguel mentioned the new amount. "First, you agree, and then you go back on your word. What kind of man are you? Besides, you're just a small part of this. A very small part. Your fair share is $400. Don't be a pig."

"A small part?" Jose Miguel had said. "You're a stranger in this area, I grew up here. You can't do this without me." He was angry, but he had to be careful. He disliked the *ingeniero*, who was more educated and lived a privileged life, but he also relied on him for work and was terrified he would call off the deal. Jose Miguel was big and strong. He gathered his courage and looked straight into the eyes of the much smaller man and said, "Five hundred."

The *ingeniero* had paused, paced around for moment, and then said, "Alright, five hundred. But no more. That's it."

Jose Miguel was thrilled, but tried not to show it. After their meeting, he had gone home to tell his wife that Ricardo would have his operation. Like Jose Miguel, his poor wife could not imagine having $500 in American money and Jose Miguel had to reassure her several times that it was true—they would soon be collecting a small fortune. He had spent the rest of that day drinking beer, thinking about his son's operation, and planning to replace the cracked windshield on his truck.

This morning, on the way to the plaza, Jose Miguel's anxiety about the transaction had returned. He was a superstitious man, afraid of many things, and had begun to fear he would be punished for what he was doing. What if something went wrong? How much trouble would there be? By the time the Land Cruiser pulled alongside his truck, Jose Miguel had decided he had no choice. He would have to trust the *ingeniero* and pray that nothing bad happened.

"Follow me," Jose Miguel said through the open window. "We can't do it here."

He drove to the edge of Estanzuela, thankful to be away from the plaza and the police station. He parked his truck among the trees on a narrow dirt road and waited for the *ingeniero* to pull up behind him.

When Jose Miguel opened the tailgate of the Land Cruiser, he saw that the rear seats had been removed and that there was plenty of space. "I'll take care of this," he told the *ingeniero*. "Watch the road and make sure no one is coming."

It didn't take long to transfer the cargo. Jose Miguel worked quickly, closed the tailgate, and gave a sigh of relief. He was glad to be finished with his part of the business.

The *ingeniero* took a bottle of beer out of his cooler and said, "*A un viaje exitoso*—to a successful trip." He offered the bottle, and Jose Miguel took a small sip. The *ingeniero* drained the remainder in a few gulps and tossed it into the brush. "I'll call you when I return," he told Jose Miguel.

The Land Cruiser disappeared down the road in a cloud of dust. Jose Miguel prayed that nothing bad happened and that the *ingeniero* returned with his $500.

"One hundred-thousand American dollars—*cash*. One hundred-thousand. One hundred-thousand American dollars," Alejandro murmured to himself as he drove west, imagining this incredible amount of money. After the cost of servicing the Land Cruiser and the small payment to Jose Miguel, the remainder of the money would be his and his alone. He didn't even have to share any of it with his Mexican acquaintance Ramiro, who had arranged the transaction. Ramiro was an agricultural engineer as well, but he worked for the Sinaloa Cartel. Just as Alejandro travelled around advising Guatemalan farmers on how to grow better crops and improve their yields, Ramiro gave the same advice to Mexican farmers—

but they were growing something else. The deal had come from high up in the cartel, and when Ramiro made the offer, Alejandro had made up his mind on the spot. Of course he would do it.

"They'll pay you on delivery in Culiacán, Mexico," Ramiro had said, and gave him an address. "Go to this place and you'll receive the money, in cash. That's how they transact business. Everything is done with hundred dollar bills."

The arrangement was clean and simple, just a one-time transaction. It was not as if Alejandro were becoming a *narco traficante*. He would do this job, collect his money, and it would be over. The idea of having $100,000 made his hands tremble on the steering wheel. He had never had so much money. At the official exchange rate, the payment was worth 780,000 Guatemalan Quetzals. In the right place in Guatemala, it might be worth almost twice as much. But why would anyone exchange American dollars for Quetzals? Quetzals were worthless. Dollars were real money. Dollars could be used anywhere to buy anything. Alejandro tried to imagine a thousand hundred-dollar bills. How much would the bills weigh? Would the money come in a bag? In a box? In a small suitcase? Would the bills be stacked and wrapped, or thrown together in a chaotic jumble? The narcos were ruthless. Would they try to cheat him? Should he stop to count the money, or would that be a sign of disrespect? Alejandro had decided he would simply take the cash and depart—what choice did he have?

The anticipation of this transaction and the money it would bring had already made Alejandro feel better about himself—bigger, stronger, and more important. He had finally stepped up to take his share of what life had to offer. He made a list of things he planned to purchase. In a few weeks, he was speaking at an environmental conference sponsored by the Ministry of Agriculture. His presentation would deal with crop rotation and the proper application of chemical fertilizers. Experts from countries in Central and South America would also be making presentations, as well as someone from California who was coming to speak about endangered species. Alejandro decided to buy a new suit and a fine pair of shoes for the occasion. He also planned to purchase a laptop computer and use it to take notes at the conference. It was important that the other speakers and those in the audience see how prosperous he was. He had no plans to tell them that his success was the result of a deal with a Sinaloa Cartel boss.

The money euphoria lasted until Alejandro arrived in the small town of San Cristobal Verapaz. The hot, dry part of Guatemala now lay behind him. Up ahead was Highway 7W and the end of the pavement. Islands of the old asphalt showed through the sea of dirt on the highway. On the road map, 7W was a double red line, indicating a main road. It appeared to be the most direct route across the northern part of Guatemala to the border crossing into Mexico. It was a Guatemalan map, however, and the double red line meant nothing. Highway? Main road? For forty years, this inaccessible region had been the stronghold of the leftist guerrillas during the country's civil war. He was about to drive the General almost 300 kilometers through the land of the ancient Maya, on a rocky dirt road that wound through rainforest valleys and climbed arid plateaus of the Sierra de los Cuchumatanes, a mountain range reaching as high as 3,700 meters. It would be a slow, rough drive in the best of weather. If he made it to the border in two days, Alejandro would be lucky. If it rained, the trip could take a week—if it rained hard, he might not make it at all. Three years ago, a landslide caused by torrential rains had destroyed part of the 7W and it had never been fully repaired. Alejandro crossed himself and again invoked the protection of Saint Christopher.

He reached the village of El Palacio as daylight began to fade. A group of old men, stooped figures walking on the side of the road, carried their work tools wrapped in blankets on their backs. A young boy pushed an ancient bicycle. In the waning light, the lush foliage dissolved into dark shadows at the edge of the road. In those places where he could still see the mountains, they melted into the clouds. The village was nothing more than a gathering of small huts with roofs of tin, clustered together in a small space carved out of the impenetrable wall of vegetation. Goats wandered about and women stood outside over open fires, stirring cooking pots. Alejandro looked at the sad little village. The Maya had such a proud history—their ancient cities were full of sculptures and murals, and they had a brilliant understanding of mathematics and astronomy. Now they were reduced to eking out a subsistence life, the poorest people in a poverty-stricken third-world country.

In the jungle, darkness comes fast and Alejandro needed a safe place to stop for the night. On the far side of the village, he found what he was looking for—a narrow space by the side of the road, hacked out of the jungle. He parked, got out to stretch his legs, and opened the rear hatch of the Land Cruiser to reassure himself that everything was in order. When he went around to the passenger side, he slid the seat back for more legroom and reclined it partway. The seat was hard and lumpy but he did his best to make himself comfortable. As the dark descended, the jungle came alive with the sounds of wild animals. The growls of the howler monkeys grew to a crescendo. Alejandro, a man of the city, heard sounds he didn't recognize. It was hours before they quieted and he was able to sleep.

The first drops of water falling on the roof of the Land Cruiser awakened him. The early morning light revealed a gray sky filled with rain.

Alejandro glanced at his watch. It was almost noon. He had been creeping along the narrow dirt road for three hours and had covered barely 35 kilometers. He was determined to keep moving, however slowly, until the weather improved. Usually the early winter weather brought a downpour in the morning, and then the sky cleared, bringing afternoon sunshine before another gusher let loose in the late evening. Today it wasn't clearing, however, and the rainfall from the grey, soggy clouds was becoming heavier. Water ran over the dirt and pooled in low spots and craters in the road. Alejandro tried to avoid the deep ruts in the center and steered toward the edge. With only a few meters of visibility, he leaned close to the windshield to get a better view between the swipes of the old wipers.

It finally became impossible to proceed. Much as he wanted to keep moving, the risk in these conditions was too great—he could drive right off the road and sink so far into the mud that even his four-wheel drive would be useless. Alejandro maneuvered the General onto a flat spot that was slightly higher than the ruts in the road. As soon as he cut the engine, the wipers stopped and the stream of fresh air blowing into the vehicle ended. In a minute, the humid air became heavy and stale. Thirty hours ago, he had left Guatemala City, and for most of that time he had been either driving or sleeping in the Land Cruiser. Now he was parked in a sea of mud, waiting for the rain to end, and feeling very claustrophobic. Alejandro squirmed in the driver's seat and tried to see out through the torrent of water running down the windshield. How long would he be trapped in this deluge? He wanted to get out, walk around, and stretch his legs. Opening the window a crack for fresh air, he felt the spray from the rain and closed it.

Alejandro hadn't eaten much since he left home the previous day and now he reached behind the seat for the cooler. He took out a potato tamale, two strips of *carne seca*, and a bottle of water and placed them on the center console. He rubbed his eyes and thought about the only thing that would make the time pass—the money. He tried to remember the details of the $100 bill he had once seen—printed in drab shades of green and gray on cream-colored paper. A wallet full of Quetzals was much more colorful, if worthless. Alejandro decided boring was alright; who cared about the color of American money? What was important was that it was easy to spend. In addition to the new suit, shoes, and computer to show off at the conference, he planned to buy a Ducati sport bike with a V-twin 1200cc displacement, and a leather jacket, helmet, and riding boots to go with it. He hadn't decided on gifts for his wife or figured out how he would explain the money to her. They needed a new stove, but he intended to buy her something else, something more personal. He had looked at gold bracelets, some set with small diamonds. By his calculation, his shopping list would consume a little more than half of the money, and he planned to save the remainder of his new wealth. Alejandro sat baking in the humid, stuffy air inside the Land Cruiser, nibbled the tamale, and listened to the rain hit the roof.

When he awoke, he looked at his watch. It was only 12:40 p.m. He had stopped only 35 minutes ago, but couldn't bear to waste any more time. He decided to resume his journey—even if he had to crawl along until the weather cleared, it would be better than sitting and doing nothing. Every kilometer travelled would bring him closer to Mexico and his money. He started the engine, felt the cool breeze of the air conditioning on his face, and eased the General forward. The vehicle travelled only a few meters in the blinding rain before Alejandro felt it lurch toward the right side of the road. Before he could react, a loud scraping sound came from the underside and the Land Cruiser pitched sideways at a sharp angle. He tapped the gas pedal and heard the whine of the transmission as the wheels spun without traction.

"*Mierda!*" he swore aloud, pounding the steering wheel with his fist. "*Mierda!*"

Alejandro opened the door, stepped out into the warm downpour, and sank deep into the mud. He slogged around to the front of the Land

Cruiser and saw that it had slid sideways off the road into a shallow ditch. The underside was hung up and the vehicle was tipped at such an angle that the right side wheels were mired deep in the trough of the ditch, while the wheels on the left side were not even touching the ground. Alejandro was no stranger to rough roads, and he did have the shovel he often used to dig the Land Cruiser out of difficult terrain, but one glance told him it would be impossible to accomplish in this sea of mud. A cable and winch were attached to the front bumper, but there was nothing he could use as an anchor. The only solution was to find pieces of wood or branches to wedge under the wheels to gain traction. He stood in the rain, his wet clothes plastered against his body, and cursed. He would have to go into the forest to forage.

Alejandro locked the General and headed for the trees. Where the road ended, the rainforest began, and as soon as he reached the dense cover of overhead leaves, vines, and tangled vegetation, the rain ceased to fall to the ground. The tallest trees, fighting for the sunlight, were as much as fifty meters high, creating an umbrella of foliage that absorbed most of the light and blocked the rainfall. Under this canopy, everything was a dim shade of green. The ground was covered with vines, rotted leaves, and bits of rock. Ferns and other plants grew in the low light, but Alejandro saw nothing he could use to wedge under his wheels. Scorpions, snakes, fire ants, and poisonous spiders lived in this debris. He bent and tucked his pant legs into his high-top boots.

The jungle was alive and feral as he began to walk. Spider monkeys pursued him, crashing through the treetops, and the shrieks of birds, the chirping of insects, and the croaking of tree frogs surrounded him. , he came upon a faint trail and began to follow it, winding his way among massive trunks of mahogany, cedar, and Santa Maria trees, and scrambling over the huge, exposed roots of kapok trees. Soon, the path disappeared and he was lost. Apprehension rippled through him as he went one way, then another, trying to retrace his route. He scanned the ground for his footprints and gazed at the massive tree trunks hoping to see something he recognized. The farther he walked, the more disoriented Alejandro became. Everything looked alike; nothing looked familiar. He fought his rising panic and tried to think clearly. How far had he come from the road? Which was the right direction? Anxiety turned to fear. He had left the General untended on the dirt road. When the rain stopped, the abandoned vehicle would attract attention. Then what? Someone would smash a window, open the back hatch, and steal everything inside. How stupid he had been to leave it unattended! He should have waited until a truck or one of the *colectivos*—small mini buses—passed the General and then offered the driver a few Quetzals to drag it out of the ditch.

He continued to a spot where a giant tree had fallen, ripping away vines and crushing smaller trees when it came down. Rain streamed in through the hole torn in the canopy above, creating a pool of water on the ground. Alejandro saw damaged branches and cursed. He had no way of cutting them from the trees. His machete was locked in the Land Cruiser along with the GPS device. How could he be so stupid? All he had was a small, useless pocketknife. He leaned against the trunk of the fallen tree, away from the rainfall. Somehow he had to find his way back to the road.

He looked down. A line of leafcutter ants marched across the forest floor, each carrying a piece of green vegetation. He glimpsed movement out of the corner of his eye and turned to look more closely. The large snake struck swiftly. Alejandro felt a sharp pain on his bicep and saw two spots of blood where the fangs had struck him. He sat in shock while the creature, at least a meter and a half long with dark triangles and a yellow zig-zag-shaped line on each side of its body, slithered away. It was a pit viper, a lance-de-fer with venom that destroys red blood cells and stops the blood from clotting. The bite would be fatal—without treatment, he would begin to bleed from the skin and eyes. Alejandro scrambled away from the fallen tree, but his legs felt clumsy and heavy. He stumbled over vines and roots and fell on the ground, gulping air and smelling the heavy musk of the rainforest floor.

Alejandro heard distant voices. When the warriors found him, they weren't gentle. They dragged him to his feet and hauled him along through the forest. Soon a noise like a waterfall grew louder, and when Alejandro and his captors burst from the vegetation into the clearing, the sound of a crowd—thousands of Mayans—reverberated around the base of what appeared to be a sacrificial pyramid.

When the people who had come from every part of the kingdom to celebrate the harvest saw Alejandro, their voices erupted into a chant, which increased in intensity as the warriors pushed him forward. Two priests, each wearing an ornate lizard headdress made of gleaming gold, stepped forward and took hold of Alejandro's arms, clasping his arms in a painful grip.

"*Ingeniero*," one of them said to Alejandro, "*Hunahpú*, the maize god, hungers for you. He will welcome our sacrifice and grant us a bountiful harvest."

Alejandro was astonished that he could understand the Mayan dialect the priest was speaking and trembled when he realized he was the sacrifice. "I can help you grow your crops," he pleaded. "Let me live, and I will teach you."

The priests ignored his appeal and began to drag him up the rough stone steps. Alejandro choked back a cry of fear as they climbed the steep side of the pyramid, ascending toward a sacrifice altar so high in the sky that it was lost in the clouds. He was naked. He looked down at his penis, shriveled in fear, and at his bare feet, which scraped against each step. The rough stone had already ripped the skin and his toes left a trail of blood. His life was lost. He would endure terrible pain before his death. First they would pierce his skin—his genitals, his lips, his tongue—and take his blood. Afterward, he could only hope they would simply press him against a stone and decapitate him. That would be the quickest death— the one he would welcome. If they used his head afterward to play one of their ballgames, he didn't care—his suffering would already be over.

As the priests dragged him upward, Alejandro began to fear something far worse than decapitation. Warriors holding spears and wearing ceremonial loincloths lined the stairway. Each man wore round earrings, a necklace of wolves' teeth, and had tattoos inked on his chest and cheeks. The line of men on the steps indicated a different death, and now Alejandro knew when it was his turn to die, he would not be cut on the sacrificial stone altar after all. Instead, they would tie his wrists to his ankles and push him down the steep stairway from the top of the pyramid. Each warrior would make sure that his body kept moving, rolling, cartwheeling and plunging down, bouncing and striking each step all the way to the base of the pyramid. How many stairs would he descend, and how many broken bones would he endure before his life spirit left his shattered body?

The procession stopped partway up the side of the pyramid. The priests on either side of him tightened their grasp, their claws digging into the flesh of his arms. They leaned in toward Alejandro and their forked lizard tongues darted out and touched his face. They weren't wearing masks. The reptiles stared at him with black, inhuman eyes and Alejandro couldn't meet their gaze. He cowered when a warrior stepped forward and pulled a stone knife from his loincloth. Did they plan to kill him here?

The warrior pushed the knife against Alejandro's forehead.

Alejandro opened his eyes and saw the interior of the Land Cruiser. He touched the painful spot on his brow and felt the slight depression where the top of the steering wheel had pressed against his forehead while he had leaned against it and slept. Had he dreamed of skidding off the road? He held his head in his hands for a moment, struggling to remember. Disjointed thoughts passed through his mind. Images of a coral snake, a Mayan blood ritual, and human-sized lizards tugged at the edge of his memory. Was there something even more terrible? Had he dreamed of his own death? He searched his brain, but the recollections were already fading, leaving him with only a vague feeling of unease.

The rain had stopped. When he opened the door, hot, humid air flooded the vehicle. He stepped out onto the wet road. Water had collected in the ruts and depressions, but the elevated spot where he had parked the Land Cruiser had kept it safe; it had not gone off the road. The rain had washed most of the SUV clean, but mud was still caked under the bumpers, in the wheel wells, and around the tires. The jungle was alive with a cacophony of noise—insects, birds, and animals, each celebrated the end of the rain. The heat and humidity descended on Alejandro and sweat began to soak through his shirt. He heard the hum of an insect and watched a blue bug with filmy wings settle on the back of his hand. There was a sharp sting before he smashed it against his skin and when he flicked it away, it left a tiny drop of blood.

The red gas cans were still tied to the roof rack. Alejandro walked around the Land Cruiser and unlocked the tailgate. When it swung open, he saw that everything was secure; nothing had been disturbed. He checked the locked box under the seat—his pistol was still there. The half-eaten tamale remained on the center console. Alejandro finished it, washed the last mouthful down with one of the Cokes from his cooler, and waited for the caffeine jolt to clear his mind.

He shook off the malaise of his dream, settled into the driver's seat, and started the engine. If the rain held off, he might complete his passage through the Cuchumatanes before nightfall.

He continued on the rough, narrow dirt road and passed through small, remote villages clinging to the sides of the mountains. Indigenous Maya—short men and women—walked along the muddy road, bent over from the loads on their backs. Most carried firewood in large baskets, but some bore heavy bags of the corn that grew on the steep slopes. Alejandro drove slowly and several times had to stop altogether and wait until wandering groups of sheep dispersed. Leaning on the horn had no effect.

Soon the road rose from the fertile lower levels of the rainforest and Alejandro began to ascend dirt switchbacks cut into the steep sides of the mountains. As he reached the exposed rock at the higher levels, the vegetation thinned to patches of bunchgrass, stunted cypress trees, and sparse pines. He passed places where cascades of water and mud had drained off during previous rainy seasons, wiping away trees, foliage, and even the dirt, leaving enormous scars of rock. Down below, he glimpsed isolated villages through the fog, nestled in the deep river valleys.

In the late afternoon, the clouds thickened again and a soft rain began to fall. After several ascents and descents, the winding, narrow dirt road finally sloped downward one last time, passing through hillsides covered with cornfields, coffee plantations, and small villages. The route levelled out and became wider. Alejandro picked up speed, came to a spot where patches of old concrete appeared in the dirt, and finally reached the place where the asphalt resumed. He was elated—after two long days, the trip across mountain highway 7W was over. Before sunset, he would be in the western city of Huehuetenango, where he had told his wife he was meeting with the coffee farmers and the Rainforest Alliance. He wasn't stopping in Huehuetenango, however, he was headed to the Mexican border.

Alejandro said a silent prayer to Saint Christopher for shepherding him through the Cuchumatanes, and wondered which saint he should call upon to bless his transaction with the Mexican drug cartel.

He spent the night on the outskirts of Huehuetenango, again sleeping in the front seat of the General. In the early morning he woke to see a clear sky. Luck was with him—the rain clouds were gone and he resumed his trip in good spirits. From the far side of Huehuetenango, it was only 55 kilometers to the city of La Mesilla and the Mexican border crossing. The last time Alejandro had crossed the border at La Mesilla it had not been pleasant. A huge shantytown and open market occupied the space between La Mesilla and the actual boundary of Guatemala. Everything imaginable was for sale, including clothing, canned goods and fruit, fireworks, bicycles and automobile parts, tools, and all the junk that was only useful in a third-world country. Trash had been dumped everywhere and when Alejandro passed through, a huge pile of plastic bottles and other garbage was on fire, sending black smoke and toxic fumes into the air. The border area itself was a squalid place filled with transients, vendors and scam artists. Outside the tiny passport control building, insistent moneychangers accosted travelers, offering to convert foreign currencies at outrageous exchange rates. Inside, an unruly crowd waiting to leave Guatemala pushed and shoved, each person trying to get to the front of the line. The fact that Alejandro was travelling on an official government passport had made no difference and he waited for hours, crushed by the tidal wave of people. Once past Immigration, the exact border was marked with a simple narrow gate. When Alejandro passed through it, they stopped him on the Mexican side and sprayed the Land Cruiser for bugs. Beyond the fumigation station was another shantytown, a better road, and a large sign—*Bienvenidos a Mexico.* Once past the sign, in the friendly land of Mexico, soldiers carrying assault rifles stopped every car and truck to question the passengers and inspect the cargo.

This time Alejandro's border crossing would be different. He had no intention of enduring the chaos at La Mesilla and couldn't risk the vehicle inspection on the Mexican side. He had something else in mind.

He had visited all of the coffee plantations in this border region several times and had travelled every road and path in the area. Alejandro had his own route into Mexico planned.

When he saw the first sign for the border, he turned off the highway and headed north toward a tiny town called El Zapote. A few kilometers before El Zapote, Alejandro came to the road leading to Kafes Guatemala—one of the largest coffee plantations in the country, thriving on the lush volcanic highland soil. As many as 150 families lived at Kafes, and most had done the same work their entire lives and had never been beyond the property line. Before he reached the Kafes entrance, Alejandro turned off onto a dirt path that ran along the perimeter of the cultivated area. He wasn't worried about attracting attention—people were accustomed to seeing the Land Cruiser from the Ministry of Interior.

Once on the path, he passed clusters of dirt-floor homes made of wood and cinder blocks, where the workers lived. Farther on, where they were spraying insecticide, Alejandro rolled up his windows. He continued past rows of mature coffee trees, almost three meters high, planted in perfect parallel lines along the hillside. The trees were just beginning show blossoms, but the fruit or "cherries," would not appear until months later in November. Alejandro drove a few kilometers along the perimeter of the plantation and finally turned off to follow a narrow rut that drifted off through the thick hillside vegetation.

Gerardo awoke to the light of the early morning sun shining through the worn canvas of his military tent. His body was damp, and the old army sleeping bag he used for a mattress was soggy with the sweat that had dripped from his body. It was usually cool during the night in these low mountains, but when yesterday's rain swept in from Mexico, it brought warmer temperatures and left the air heavy with humidity.

"Diego, it's your turn to get the water," Gerardo murmured while he lay on his back and listened to the sounds of the birds outside. When there was no reply, he said, "Hey, are you awake?" He rolled over and pushed away the mosquito net draped around him and saw he was alone in the tent. He went outside wearing only his olive-green army underwear, and stood in a leafy clearing on the edge of the coffee plantation. He shouted, "Diego?" The birds in the treetops—toucans, parrots, and parakeets—shrieked in response, but no human voice responded. Gerardo went back inside the tent, put his hand on Diego's sleeping bag, and felt that it was dry. Diego's rifle, pistol, and pack were missing and he knew he wouldn't see him again. Gerardo whispered, "*Dios te acompañe*—God be with you," and pulled on his pants.

Gerardo had no radio and no way of contacting his platoon leader to report the desertion. He had another 48 hours to wait until relief came, but it didn't matter, there was no emergency. Someone else would come to replace Diego and eventually he too would take his weapons and disappear in the middle of the night. It was a common occurrence. Most Guatemalans served two or three years in the National Army or the Federal Police Force, learned the skills they needed, and then walked away to become cartel soldiers.

Gerardo could earn a hundred times his government paycheck if he went to work for the *narcos*, and each time he put on the uniform he had been required to purchase with his own money, he was reminded of just how little he was paid. He might have already deserted, but he was afraid of what his brother Felipe would do. Once, when Gerardo had talked about joining the cartel, his brother had become furious. "No you won't," Felipe had said, "I forbid it. Not now. Not ever." He had shaken his fist at Gerardo and continued, "They're killers, animals. Stay away from those people. If you join them, I'll come and drag you back."

It seemed impossible that he and his clear-eyed, self-confident brother had come from the womb of the same mother—a barely literate woman who had worked most of her life cleaning the toilets and washrooms at the American Embassy in Guatemala City. It was true that he and his brother looked alike, but the similarity ended there. From the time they were children, Felipe had always been a leader and Gerardo had always been a follower. Gerardo was ordinary and unexceptional, while his older brother was already a rising star in the military. Gerardo had dropped out of school and kicked around the streets. His brother had graduated from the Escuela Politécnica—Guatemala's military academy—and had become a member of the Kaibiles—the Guatemalan Special Forces. Gerardo had reluctantly joined the army because he couldn't find a job, while Felipe had been selected to go to the United States to train with the Texas Army National Guard. Gerardo's brother would make it to the top of the military. He had light colored skin—much lighter than Gerardo's—and that would make it easier. Someday Felipe would become a rich and powerful general, have a beautiful wife, and live in a grand house. He would have important friends—some might even be cartel leaders. All he had to do was live long enough.

When Gerardo last heard from his brother, he was fighting with a newly formed elite military unit trying to regain control of the area in Quiché, on the Mexican border, where Los Zetas and the Mara Salvatrucha gang had taken over. The violence had become horrific, and after Los Zetas beheaded 26 workers on a farm, his brother had fumed, "Our country can't go on like this. Someone has to drive these vermin out, and we're gonna do it."

Felipe was right, Guatemala was lawless; violence and killing had become a way of life and everyone said *la vida no vale nada en Guatemala*—life is worth nothing in Guatemala. Gerardo was doing his part, however insignificant. For a week, he and Diego had been camped at the edge of a large coffee ranch in the Huehuetenango highlands, guarding a deserted path that dead-ended at a shallow creek along the Mexican border. They were supposed to be helping the army correct what it called "border security deficiencies." To the north, human and drug traffickers, gang members, and migrant workers crossed the border at will. To the south, legitimate travelers passed over the crossing at La Mesilla. Between north and south lay the vast coffee plantations and the deserted path Gerardo was now guarding alone. In all the time he had been on duty, he had not seen a single person, only snakes, insects, birds, and wandering goats.

Gerardo put on his sweat-stained uniform but didn't bother with his boots because they were too small; he could walk to the creek without them. He buckled his belt and felt the weight of the old Star nine-millimeter pistol hanging in the holster. He didn't bother to take his rifle, though he was required to carry it with him at all times. That was just one of many stupid things the Army said he was supposed to do, but he chose to ignore because it was too much trouble. He picked up the empty water bucket and headed toward the creek. It was a good morning to take a bath and wash his filthy uniform.

Alejandro followed the faint path through the thick vegetation. It was exactly as he remembered, and the creek could not be far away. Suddenly, a lone soldier carrying a bucket emerged from nowhere. From his startled look, the man was as surprised to see the Land Cruiser as Alejandro was to see him. Alejandro stopped and peered at him through the windshield. The soldier was barefoot and shabby—probably a deserter. When he dropped his bucket and reached for the gun hanging from his belt, Alejandro reacted without thinking. He jammed his foot hard against the accelerator and the four-wheel drive propelled the Land Cruiser forward. Before the soldier could fire his pistol, the front bumper struck him head-on. In a panic, Alejandro felt the bump when his new tires rolled over the soldier's body, but kept his foot on the gas. Something dragged along under the General, but he kept moving.

Alejandro stopped when he reached the creek and sat trembling, staring at the water. When he finally got out of the Land Cruiser, he checked the front end first, but it already had so many dents that he couldn't see any new damage. He walked around the vehicle and bent down, fearful of what he would find underneath. There was no sign of the soldier's body, but the handle of the man's bucket had caught on the muffler. Alejandro climbed up onto the roof of the Land Cruiser, looked back over the path, and was relieved that he didn't see a crumpled body. Should he walk back and look for the soldier? Did he really want to find a dead body? The answer was no. What was done was done, and he couldn't bring the man back to life. Alejandro had acted in self-defense—if he hadn't run him down, the man would have shot him. It was time to move on.

He returned to the driver's seat, shifted into low gear, and drove into the middle of the creek. Runoff from the previous day's rainstorm had raised the water level, and it was wider and deeper than he remembered. He watched the odometer as the vehicle bounced and pitched from side to side, passing over rocks and sinking into depressions in the bed of the creek. He was supposed to travel about 100 meters upstream—he searched for the large kapok tree that marked the spot. As he remembered it, the tree was quite tall, and should be easily seen from a distance. As the Land Cruiser crept up the middle of the creek, Alejandro saw nothing as distinctive as a kapok tree and stopped to get another reading on his GPS. He was at the precise latitude and longitude, but saw no tree and no entry into the jungle on the far side. Alejandro searched his memory. Could he be mistaken? It had only been two years since someone had shown him the place where the kapok tree marked the path across the border. He remembered it so clearly. He had stood in the creek and decided that if he ever had to cross into Mexico secretly, this would be the place to do it. How could a tree that had stood out, meters taller than anything around it, disappear?

Alejandro opened the door, stepped into the creek, and felt the cool water seep into his boots. He checked his GPS yet again. What was he missing? He waded to the far side and, as he approached the bank, he saw it in the water. Someone had cut down the tree and all that remained was the stump and the mass of thick roots, submerged under the high water. Alejandro went back to the Land Cruiser, grabbed his machete, and struggled through the mud and up the bank of the creek. He hacked away at the vegetation, cutting through the thin ropes that held several small trees down and obscured the view of the path from the creek. "*Si puedo,*" he exclaimed, and pumped his fist in the air. It took him less than ten minutes to clear an opening wide enough for the General.

The wheels spun for a moment as he drove up onto the bank and plowed through the tangled growth. After a few meters, the track into Mexico became visible and appeared well travelled. As Alejandro proceeded, plastic bottles and other discarded debris told him that this crossing point had become a regular route across the border. He continued for several kilometers until the path came to a dead-end at a shallow ditch. On the other side was a paved road; Alejandro drove across the ditch and entered Mexico.

The General's tank was near empty. Alejandro stopped and took down one of the red plastic gas containers. After he filled the tank, he extracted the second of the three bottles of beer from his cooler. "*Bienvenido a Mexico,*" he said aloud and held the bottle up in an imaginary toast. The beer was warm, but he enjoyed it anyway. He had overcome the harsh Guatemalan roads and crossed the border safely with his cargo. Now all he had to do was survive the trip through Mexico.

Ahead of him lay 2,500-kilometers on Mexico Highway 200, the main road along the Pacific Coast. The trip north would take Alejandro past Acapulco, Puerto Vallarta, and Mazatlan before reaching Culiacán. The condition of the road itself had been the challenge in Guatemala, but that was not the big risk on the journey ahead. Highway 200 was a winding, two-lane paved road. The real danger was what Alejandro might encounter. He had been warned not to travel at night. Drunk drivers, livestock, pedestrians, and unlighted farm equipment were some of the lesser hazards. The real threat, day or night however, was robbery and hijacking, and he had read several reports of travelers coming upon roadblocks set by bandits armed with machetes and machine guns, decked out in bulletproof vests draped with hand grenades. Alejandro planned to keep moving and cover about 800 kilometers. By evening, he hoped to reach Acapulco.

The beer left Alejandro with a slight buzz. His stomach was empty and he rummaged through his cooler for something to eat. He found two dry tamales, which he washed down with his last Coca Cola. He would have to drive today without eating and purchase food when he stopped for the night. Before heading north, Alejandro unlocked the box under the drivers' seat, took out the Colt .45, chambered a round, and laid the gun on his passenger seat. It gave him some comfort, although he hoped he wouldn't have to use it. If the worst happened and he was waylaid, he had prepared a story, one he hoped would save him.

After fifty kilometers, Alejandro came up behind three semi-trailer trucks moving in a convoy. They must have been empty, because they were barreling along, driving in the center of the road, and moving fast. He followed behind them for another 100 kilometers, watching the trucks cutting corners on every curve of the road and hoping no one was approaching in the opposite direction. When the trucks finally turned off, he drove on alone. An ocean breeze was blowing and he opened the windows and let it cool him. He passed a big billboard with pictures of Mexico's three most wanted criminals, all cartel leaders. Their faces had been covered with black paint.

Blanca ran her tongue over the little silver ring that pierced the center of her lower lip and stared through the binoculars. Standing next to the old pickup, under the hot Mexican sun, she had a good view of a stretch of Highway 200. She scanned the road for oncoming targets, and thought for a moment about her *vida loca*—her crazy life. Everyone in Mexico talked about going *al otro lado*, to the other side, but she had come south from the mean streets of East Los Angeles to Mexico. Her mother had been a member of the Dreamers, and Blanca grew up sleeping on a filthy mattress on the floor of their gang house. She was twelve when her mother abandoned her, and Blanca quickly learned to run drugs on the streets to survive. Three years later, she went through the courting in—the Dreamers' initiation. They gave her a choice—fuck every man in the gang or submit to a beating. Blanca didn't particularly like sex with men, so she chose the beating. She was a big girl, a very big girl, and the initiation didn't go quite as planned. Before they knocked her senseless, she managed to break one gang member's nose and take down another with a direct kick to his groin. After the initiation, Blanca became a regular member of the Dreamers and they left her alone—no one tried to fuck her or fuck with her. As she grew older, she became as strong as many of the men and as fearless as any of them. They all told her, "*Blanca, tu tienes heuvos!*— you got balls!" She chose the women she liked and punished those who spurned her. When the one she loved was arrested and deported, Blanca followed her to Mexico, only to watch her die of an overdose.

Now, at twenty-three, she led a small gang of women who robbed travelers on the Mexican roads. They had begun jacking vehicles on Highway 200 between Acapulco and Puerto Vallarta, in the Mexican state of Michoacan until La Familia Michoacana, the local crime syndicate, put an end to it. La Familia was the law and the power in Michoacan and wouldn't permit any disturbances caused by small-time road bandits. When La Familia did a highway stop, it was to seize trucks and SUVs they could use to haul contraband and people, not to steal wallets and personal electronic gear. La Familia made gruesome examples of troublemakers on the road, and they called it *corpse messaging*. Blanca began to have nightmares about La Familia soldiers carving their initials in her flesh before dismembering her, and decided to move her gang farther south, into the state of Oaxaca near the Guatemalan border. It was safer there, although the people travelling the highway were much poorer.

A vehicle appeared in the distance and she hit the door of the truck with the palm of her hand. "Margarita," she said, "someone's coming. Get the cows." Blanca had found that placing animals on the road was an effective way of stopping oncoming traffic, although one time a truck had refused to yield and had plowed into the stupid beasts, killing two and splattering animal parts and blood all over the highway.

Margarita led several cows out onto the highway and put heavy rocks on their halters to keep them from moving. Blanca positioned the pickup behind the cows, checked her shotgun, and waited.

Up ahead, Alejandro saw animals in the middle of the road, and as he got closer, he saw that they were cows. Why were they standing there? He slowed and leaned on his horn. When they didn't move aside, he stopped. By the time he saw the pickup truck blocking the highway behind them, it was too late. Before he could reach across the seat to grab his .45, a big, tough-looking woman appeared and pointed a shotgun at him through the passenger side window.

She opened the door, took the pistol from the seat, and stuck it into her waistband. "Out," she said, waving the shotgun at him.

Alejandro's pulse jumped and his mind raced. This was what he had feared the most—Mexican highway bandits. Was it just this one woman? She looked young, in her twenties, but hard and cruel. She had a short, thick body and gang tattoos covered her face, neck, and arms. There was a determination in her eyes that he was afraid to challenge. While he stared, another woman—a girl, really—came around to his side of the Land Cruiser holding an automatic weapon that looked too big for her small hands. She opened his door and held the gun barrel inches from his face. "Give me the keys," she said, "and get out."

Alejandro pulled the keys from the ignition. As he slid out of the Land Cruiser, the girl hit him hard in the thigh with the butt of her weapon. A wave of pain shot through his body. He fell on the ground and she grabbed his keys from his hand.

Blanca came around to look at the man lying on the ground. His old Land Cruiser had some kind of Guatemalan government insignia. "*Maldita sea*," she swore aloud. Guatemalans were poorer than Mexicans. The ancient .45 pistol might be the only prize. She stood over the Guatemalan and said, "Gimme your wristwatch, wallet, and everything you have in your pockets."

He handed his watch to her. Blanca looked at it. It was cheap and made of black plastic and might be worth fifty pesos. He stood up, favoring his leg, and gave her his wallet, a pocketknife and a few colorful bills of Guatemalan money.

Blanca stuffed everything into a bag she carried slung over her shoulder. "What else?" she said.

"That's all I have, I'm not a tourist. I don't have anything valuable. I'm here on government business."

"I don't give a shit what kind of business you're on," Blanca said, and leaned into the SUV and opened the center console. She tossed out the vehicle's registration papers and found a GPS and a small set of binoculars, which she added to her bag of plunder. "Let's see what you have in the back," she said, and walked around to open the rear hatch.

The pain in his thigh was excruciating as Alejandro hobbled around to the back of the Land Cruiser. When the woman with the tattoos opened the hatch, he closed his eyes and said a silent prayer.

Blanca saw a large rectangular metal cage. She looked closely, but saw nothing inside but wood chips and moss. She pulled the heavy cage toward her and shook it.

Nothing.

Blanca shook it again, and was surprised to see a lizard nestled in the wood chips. When it moved, she saw that it was enormous. She had seen hundreds of geckos, they were all over Mexico and she knew what they looked like. This creature was not a gecko. It was almost as long as her arm and half of it was tail. It was fierce looking, with a wide, flat head, thick short legs, and feet with five clawed toes. The reptile was black with spots of yellow color and its skin was bumpy, almost as if it were covered with beads. The thick black tail had yellow bands around it. Blanca had never seen anything like it.

The lizard watched Blanca with black eyes. Its pink forked tongue flicked in and out of its mouth.

Blanca was awestruck. "*Lagarto?*" she asked the Guatemalan. "*Iguana negra?*"

"It's not a black iguana," Alejandro said. "It's a rare lizard that I'm taking it to the Parque Zoologico in Mexico City for a breeding program." His story rolled easily off his tongue and he was thankful he had planned it in advance—it sounded genuine. "That's my job, I take care of lizards."

Blanca leaned toward the cage and looked more closely at the reptile. It looked so badass.

Margarita came around to the back of the Land Cruiser, still holding the assault rifle. "*Guácala!*" she uttered when she saw the lizard in the cage, and backed away. "I hate lizards and snakes."

"It's nothing to be afraid of," Blanca said. She tapped the side of the metal cage with her knuckles. "*Hola, lagarto.* I'm Blanca." She was determined to show Margarita how brave she was.

The lizard raised itself up on its front legs, swayed from side to side, and hissed.

"Hah," Blanca said. "Look, it's afraid of me."

"It's ugly," Margarita said.

"It's just a big black lizard," Blanca said. "It's nothing to be afraid of. Watch, I can touch it."

Apprehension spread across Margarita's face, and she backed further away from the cage. "Don't let it out," she said.

"Watch this." Blanca propped her shotgun against the rear bumper of the Land Cruiser then stuck her index finger through the metal lattice of the cage and wiggled it.

The lizard swayed and hissed again.

"That's right. You stupid lizard," she said. "I'm Blanca—you don't scare me." She glanced at Margarita, then pushed her finger in as far as she could and tried to touch the reptile.

The lizard struck fast, burying its teeth in Blanca's fingertip. "Aiee!" She screamed and tried to pull her hand away. The lizard held tight while venom from the glands in the base of his grooved teeth drained into her soft flesh. Margarita stepped toward the cage and pointed the barrel of her gun at the lizard.

"Don't," Alejandro said. "You'll shoot her finger off." He grabbed Blanca's arm and yanked it away from the cage. She screamed in agony when her finger ripped free of the lizard's teeth and left a piece of her flesh in its jaws.

"It bit me," Blanca cried. "It hurts." Blood dripped from the torn finger.

Pain spread across her face, replacing the defiance. "The lizard's poison will affect your central nervous system," Alejandro told her. "Do you even know what your central nervous system is?"

"My whole arm is starting to hurt." Tears rolled down Blanca's cheeks. "It burns! My heart's pounding."

Margarita dropped the assault rifle and held Blanca's finger in her hand.

"The pain will become unbearable, and then you'll start to vomit," Alejandro said, and smiled at her. "In a few hours you'll be paralyzed and won't be able to breathe." He took his .45 from Blanca's waistband and pulled the small bag holding his possessions off her shoulder. "How do you like that?" He turned to her accomplice and said, "You've got an hour to find a doctor before she dies."

The two *bandidas* ran to their pickup. Alejandro had read that the lizard's bite could be very painful and the venom would wreak havoc on a human body, but if Blanca didn't die of fear, she would survive. He couldn't believe she had been stupid enough to stick her finger into the cage. He smiled as he imagined their terror while they searched for a doctor.

"Serves you right," Alejandro said.

When the *bandidas* sped away, Alejandro moved the rocks holding the cow's halters and herded the animals off the highway. He drove the Land Cruiser to the side of the road with the back gate still open and walked around to look more closely at the lizard. He had checked on it several times during the three days since Jose Miguel had placed the cage in the back of the General, but each time, the creature had remained hidden in the moss and wood chips. Now it was fully revealed and this was the first opportunity Alejandro had to get a good look at the fabled Motagua Valley beaded lizard. It was a beautiful and fearsome looking creature, more remarkable than the pictures he had found on the Internet. When he leaned in for a closer view, he saw a tiny shred of Blanca's flesh and some of her blood at the edge of the creature's mouth.

Six months ago, Alejandro wasn't even aware beaded lizards existed, although he had heard of their venomous cousin, the Gila Monster. During the time he waited for Jose Miguel to capture the reptile, he had done some research and found that there were beaded lizards from Mexico and from Guatemala. The ones from Guatemala—estimated to total less than two hundred—lived in the foothills of the Motagua River Valley. They were the rarest and most endangered species on the planet and their scarcity made them almost priceless on the black market. Alejandro had found dozens of exaggerated and fantastic tales about the venomous bite of this lizard, called "the pit bull of reptiles." The Mayans who lived in the Motagua River Valley believed that the lizard attracted the electricity of the sky, and that any spot where lightning struck was a place where a Motagua Lizard was hiding underground. A more recent fable described the lizard as a demon, a magical creature that brought a curse of ill fortune and death to anyone who held it captive.

Studying the extraordinary creature in the back of his Land Cruiser, he wondered if $100,000 was a fair price for such a rare and beautiful reptile. Everyone knew that the cartel bosses collected exotic animals like snow leopards, black panthers, and even rare monkeys. This lizard would make a great addition to some drug lord's collection. Should he have bargained for a larger payment? Were the *narcos* in Culiacán cheating him? He thought about the money he had promised Jose Miguel, and admitted to himself that the sale of the lizard to the cartel would not have been possible without him. After all, it was Jose Miguel who knew where to look for the beaded lizards and it was a miracle that he had actually found one. Alejandro felt a pang of guilt at how he had treated Jose Miguel. He decided to pay him a bonus when he returned home.

After the incident with the two *bandidas*, Alejandro continued his trip north with confidence. He had lost his fear of the road. All the bad things had already happened. What could stop him now?

He spent the first night near Acapulco, the second night outside of Puerto Vallarta, and on the morning of the third day, he set out at sunrise for Culiacán. Near Mazatlan, 225 kilometers from Culiacán, he picked up Federal Highway 15, a modern four-lane road that ran from Mexico City to the U.S. Border. Now the General was speeding along and Alejandro no longer had to worry about poor pavement, livestock, or road bandits. Soon the traffic became heavier and the PEMEX gas stations more frequent. He had reached civilization. When he saw the green and white highway sign that indicated CULIACÁN – 20 KM, he pulled off the road. He was now in the state of Sinaloa—the cradle of the Mexican drug cartels and home of the best opium poppies in the world. Jubilation swept through him. His journey was almost complete. In an hour, the *narcos* would have their beaded lizard and he would have his money.

Alejandro took the last beer out of the cooler. He popped the top and turned to the cage in the back of the Land Cruiser. "*Salud,* lizard, welcome to Mexico," he said, and drained the bottle. A warm beer had never tasted better. He took out the address and directions he had been given and tried to picture the home of a cartel boss. They lived in a neighborhood of palatial homes called Tierra Blanca and he imagined arriving at a compound located on a hillside with a beautiful view. It would have high walls around it for security purposes and armed guards would stop him outside a fortified gate. As soon as he told them he had the lizard, they would escort him to a large and beautiful house. In the front, expensive cars—Ferraris, Porsches, Lamborghinis—would be lined up. In the back, beautiful women wearing bikinis, gold jewelry, and diamonds would be lying around a swimming pool—an infinity pool—on luxurious lounges under white umbrellas. Perhaps a tiger or a cheetah would be pacing back and forth in a cage nearby. There would be excitement when word of the arrival of the reptile spread through the compound, and Alejandro imagined standing quietly while a crowd gathered to see it. That would be the end to his trip to Mexico. He doubted they would ask him to share a drink by the pool, and even if the invitation were extended, he decided he would decline. He planned to drive back to Mazatlan immediately, find the finest hotel, and take the best room. He needed a bath and a shave, and then a woman to massage his aching back muscles. He wanted a wonderful meal from room service and then, after stuffing himself, he would call for another woman, a first-class Mexican beauty to spend the night with him. Best of all, the cost wouldn't matter; he would pay for everything from his vast fortune of hundred-dollar bills. In the morning, before heading back to Guatemala, he planned to deposit his new wealth in a Mexican bank.

He followed the traffic signs into Culiacán. The city lay between the Pacific Ocean and the Sierra Madres saw the silhouette of the mountains in the distance. He entered from the south, on Boulevard Militar. The wide thoroughfare, lined with old palm trees, was jammed with traffic. Near the center of the town he passed several white government buildings and a beautiful church. He drove for kilometers past car dealerships featuring high-end four-wheel drive vehicles and exotic sports cars. Beyond the dealerships, he saw showrooms filled with boats and motorcycles. He had arrived in the drug capital of Mexico; nothing like this existed in Guatemala. In the distance Alejandro saw green hills studded with homes and wondered if that was the enclave of the drug bosses.

He drove behind a bus belching black smoke for a few more kilometers while he checked his directions and looked at the street signs. When he finally turned off onto Avenida Urales, he was already beyond the center of the city and the beautiful homes in the hills were behind him. He was now headed into an old, rundown part of Culiacán with vacant lots and piles of garbage and debris. He turned right and then left on several streets, each narrower and more dismal than the last. Finally, he came to a grimy street called Calle Fresnillo. A mangy dog lay in front of an empty *taqueria* with vacant sidewalk tables. He continued down the street, past cement walls painted with graffiti and small, single-story buildings with heavy iron grates covering the windows and doors. At the end of the second block, Alejandro passed the gutted shell of an automobile at the side of the street. At an open garage with a sign that said *Transmissiones Automaticas*, he saw the address he had been given. On the street, two men wearing grease-stained T-shirts and dirty overalls bent over the engine of a pickup truck. They didn't look like they were working on it, and as he approached, they levelled pistols at him.

"*No, no dispara*—don't shoot," Alejandro called out. He stopped and held both hands outside the window. "I'm here to deliver the lizard."

The two men said nothing and approached the Land Cruiser.

"The lizard," Alejandro repeated. Moving slowly, he opened the door, got out, and held his hands up. He looked up at the security camera with the blinking red light mounted above the entrance to the garage and said, "I brought the beaded lizard."

A third man came out of the garage holding a cell phone. He looked at Alejandro with dark, humorless eyes and said, "Open the back."

Alejandro walked around behind the General and one of the men followed him, pointing his weapon at Alejandro's back. He unlocked the hatch and let it swing up. "I brought it from Guatemala," he said, and rapped his knuckles against the cage.

The man with the cell phone stared at the pile of wood chips. "Where is it?" he asked.

"It's underneath."

"Show me," the man said.

Alejandro shook the cage until the lizard's head appeared. Alejandro shook harder, and the lizard showed its entire body, began to hiss, and moved its head from side to side.

The man with the cell phone punched in some numbers, held it to his ear, and after a moment said, "*Esta aqui*—it's here."

The sound of a racing engine attracted Alejandro's attention. He looked up to see a black Cadillac Escalade coming toward them down the center of Calle Fresnillo. It was moving fast and his gaze was drawn from the shining silver grill to the gun barrels that appeared when the dark tinted windows came down. He heard the loud rattle of automatic weapons from the Escalade and the answering barrage from the men standing near him on the street. Alejandro was caught in the crossfire as bullets slammed into everything around him. The windows of the Land Cruiser disintegrated and the three men collapsed in an explosion of blood and flesh. Alejandro felt a hot, searing pain surge through his body and saw red bloodstains spreading across his shirt. Before he fell to the pavement, he remembered the curse of the damned lizard.

II | THE LIZARD

He is one of only three venomous lizards on the face of the earth and folklore is filled with myths of this monster and the pain, suffering, and death that he brings. He has many names: Guatemalan beaded lizard; Motagua Valley beaded lizard; *Escorpión*; and *El Niño Dormido* – "The Sleeping Baby." His studded skin is like armor, consisting of tiny beads, each of which contains a minute piece of bone. His look is unique—his skin is black, marked with mottled patches of yellow, and he has a strong tail with distinct yellow and black bands.

His Latin name is *Heloderma horridum charlesbogerti*. Heloderma means studded skin; horridum means horrible. Charles Bogert was an early curator of the Department of Herpetology of the American Museum of Natural History.

Discovered in 1984 by an agricultural laborer in Guatemala, he is regarded as a living fossil, the survivor of an ancestry that has lived relatively unchanged for as long as 100 million years, beginning before the existence of many of the dinosaurs. His lifespan is nearly fifty years.

The beaded lizard spends his entire life roaming the hot, tropical dry forest in the Motagua River Valley in southeastern Guatemala, isolated from the rest of the world by massive cloud covered mountains and rainforest valleys. His habitat is disappearing and he is facing extinction. It is estimated that there are no more than 400 of his species remaining.

III | THE CUIZA

Dedo dove into his pool and began his morning workout—fifty laps in a fifty-meter pool. He loved the feeling of gliding through the cool water, following the lines of azure tile that ran along the bottom. He savored the rush of endorphins that came after he worked his muscles to exhaustion and enjoyed the burn in his lungs when he stood in the shallow end gasping for breath. Dedo had once imagined he would be a great swimmer, maybe even world-class, and sometimes he wondered what kind of life that would have been. Instead, he had gone to the London School of Economics and had become a world-class money manager. Well, no, not exactly. Dedo might not be a world-class money manager, but he managed a world-class amount of money—for the Sinaloa drug cartel. His real name was Pella Delgado, but his friends called him Dedo—the finger—and everyone else referred to him as *El Dedo de Oro*—Goldfinger.

On the eighth lap, his reverie was interrupted by a musical version of *Money* by K. T. Oslin, coming from the surround-sound system installed at the pool. The tune was the emergency ring tone on his cell phone—someone was calling him on his secure line. Only a few people had access to the number and no one called unless there was a crisis. Dedo swam to the side, his heart racing from more than physical exertion.

He grabbed the phone lying on his towel and said, "What?"

"We just got hit by Los Aztecas. They machine-gunned three of our men at the garage on Calle Fresnillo."

"So?" Dedo exploded. "I'm in the middle of my workout and you're calling to tell me about a gun battle? On this line? I don't care who was shot. Not my problem."

Luis' voice faltered for a moment. "Sorry, Dedo," he said. "Someone else was involved. The Guatemalan just arrived and he was cut down, too. He brought the lizard."

"*Maldita sea*," Dedo exclaimed. "Is it alive?"

"I don't know. It's in a cage and the Cuiza's checking it out right now. Things are a mess here—a lot of blood. The *Policia Federal* showed up and we told them to wait down the street at a *taqueria*. What should we do about the Guatemalan's body?"

"I don't care," Dedo said. "Let the Federales have him. Just make sure the lizard is safe and bring it up here."

"Right," Luis said.

Dedo disconnected, tossed his cell phone onto a lounge, and swam underwater to the end of the pool. He took a breath and resumed his laps, trying to lose himself again in the rhythm of his effort, but the serenity of the workout had been spoiled. *The lizard*! He couldn't call Los Angeles and tell Felix it had been slaughtered during a gun battle. That would be a huge embarrassment, after first searching for someone who could capture a Motagua Valley beaded lizard and then waiting three months for it to arrive in Culiacán. The turf war between the cartels wasn't something Dedo got directly involved in, but if the Juárez people had shot up the lizard, he would teach them and their hired killers, Los Aztecas, a lesson. By the time he started his 25th lap, Dedo had come up with a plan to hack into a Juárez Cartel bank account in Chicago and withdraw tens of millions of dollars.

The Cuiza sat in the back of the Hummer while it sped through the hills above Culiacán. He was never allowed to sit in the front, but today he didn't care—he was hanging over the back seat, looking at the amazing lizard in the cage. Never in his life had the Cuiza seen anything like it. "Chik, chik, chik," he said.

"Yeah," the driver said, watching the Cuiza in the rearview mirror. "I'll bet you're excited. Big lizard, huh? Not like your little geckos, is it?"

"Hey Cuiza," Luis said from the passenger seat. "You related to that thing?"

"Chik, chik, chik." The Cuiza made the gecko sound, the series of three chirps, trying to get the lizard's attention. It didn't matter what the men said; he didn't care what they thought. In fact, the Cuiza didn't like most people. A few helped him when he needed something to eat or a place to sleep, but most just ignored him. Some were even cruel. Lizards and geckos were his true friends—they were the most important things in his life.

"Fucking Aztecas," the driver said.

"Good thing the lizard's in one piece," Luis said, glancing in the back. "Or Dedo would be really pissed."

"Poor fucking Guatemalan," the driver said.

"Chik, chik, chik," the Cuiza said.

The beaded lizard rested on top of the wood chips. It raised its head and looked at the Cuiza. Its pink forked tongue flicked in and out.

When the Hummer arrived at Dedo's gate, men wearing bulletproof vests and carrying AK47's appeared. Luis lowered the tinted window and leaned out. "We brought the lizard," he said.

One of the guards opened the back and looked at the creature inside the cage. "*Es feísimo*—ugly as sin." He scratched his unshaven face, and closed the hatch.

The Hummer passed through the gate and continued inside the wall for a kilometer down a smooth road of close-set pavers lined by beautiful old Montezuma Cypress trees. A flock of Boat-Billed Flycatchers with bright yellow bodies took flight as the car sped past. When they parked in front of the house, the Cuiza was the first one out of the Hummer. He ran around to the back and waited for Luis to unload the cage.

Dedo opened the front door of the house and came out to join them. "Is it alright?" he asked. "It better be alive."

"Chik, chik, chik," the Cuiza said.

"Yeah, it's alive," Luis said. "The Guatemalan was just about cut in half and his Land Cruiser took about thirty bullets, but the cage was down low and wasn't hit." He opened the back of the Hummer, pulled out the cage, and placed it on the ground. "Take a look."

Dedo bent down and looked at the reptile. "This is the rarest lizard in the world?" he said. "This is what Felix is so excited about?" Dedo stared at the black-and-yellow lizard with yellow rings on its tail.

The lizard's round beady eyes stared back at Dedo.

"I need a favor," Felix Cabrera had told Dedo when he called from Los Angeles. "A big favor."

"What?" Dedo asked. He always answered calls from Felix, because Felix was important. He directed the Cartel's cocaine distribution in the United States and besides, Dedo liked him.

"You have to find a lizard for me."

"A lizard?" Dedo said. "Are you joking?"

"No, and it's not just any lizard. I'm after something called a Motagua Valley beaded lizard. You've got contacts in Guatemala, right?"

"I know some people."

"This lizard only exists in one place in the world. In Guatemala. In the Motagua River Valley. Ever hear of it?"

"Never."

"Well, it's in the northeast, near the border with Honduras. Can you find someone to go out and look for one? Someone who lives in that area?

"Reptiles aren't exactly my field of expertise," Dedo had said. "You plan on using them to bring in drugs?"

"No, these lizards are so rare, they're on the endangered list. They're priceless. This lizard hasn't changed in millions of years. I want one, and I don't care what it costs."

"I can make some calls and see what I can do. No promises."

"You're a smart guy, Dedo. If anyone can figure out how to find one, it's you."

"I'll let you know."

"I would appreciate that. Just so you know, there are Mexican beaded lizards too. They're rare, but not as rare as the ones from Guatemala. I don't want a Mexican beaded lizard. It has to come from the Motagua River Valley."

"Will I know the difference?"

"If it comes from Guatemala, it's the real thing."

Three months later, Felix was thrilled when Dedo called with the message that a Guatemalan beaded lizard had been found and was soon to be delivered to Culiacán. When Felix asked about the cost, Dedo said it was a gift. Felix recognized the gesture as a sign of respect, a sign of how far he had come. He grew up in Fontana, California, a hot, dusty rail hub east of Los Angeles and spent his summers on the road riding with his father, a cross-country truck driver. He had planned to attend a community college, but as soon as he was old enough, his father insisted that Felix hire out as a freight driver to help support the family. His first job was driving an old Freightliner to Chicago once a week for a small shipping company.

Felix had been lucky—he was in the right place at the right time. The place was a truck stop on the California-Arizona border, where someone approached him and asked where he was headed. When Felix said Chicago, the man, a Mexican-American like himself, asked if he would deliver a package to a place near O'Hare airport. He gave Felix an address and told him he would be paid $100 for the delivery. This happened in 1995, which was the right time, because the Mexican cartels were just beginning to set up their own networks and were replacing the Colombians as the big drug distributors in the United States.

Now, twenty years later, Felix lived in an upper-middle-class neighborhood in Santa Ana and owned a thriving business, transporting frozen chickens in a small fleet of tractor-trailers. He was an average looking man, unremarkable in every way. Nothing about him hinted that he was also the kingpin of a cocaine distribution network that he had started in the poor, immigrant neighborhoods along the trucking corridors of Southern California, and which now stretched like a vast spider web across the entire United States. In the process, he had become incredibly wealthy. Felix Cabrera was a self-made man, living the American dream.

His favorite border crossing was Calexico, in Imperial County in the Southeast corner of California, across from the Mexican city of Mexicali. Felix ran a small army of border lookouts and drivers, many of whom were Americans, and he had one rule. Actually, he had many rules, but the most important one was, once you begin as a driver, you cannot quit. In the beginning, Felix had to shoot a few recalcitrant drivers, but once word got around, no one argued and no one quit.

He used a fleet of SUVs and cars with custom-made hidden compartments. To foil the dogs, Felix shrink-wrapped the cocaine along with garlic or mustard, and covered the packages with axle grease. Each shipment was relatively small, between 300 - 600 pounds, to reduce losses in the event of a seizure, but the cumulative activity brought more than a ton of cocaine into the United States each month. On the American side, Felix stored it in stash houses, repackaged it with wrapping materials purchased at Costco, and distributed the white powder to a nationwide network of street and prison gangs, organized crime syndicates, and low-level drug entrepreneurs. The price of a kilo was $18,000 on the street in Los Angeles and escalated as it moved east. In New York, it was worth $25,000. Felix was a detail-oriented businessman who managed every level of his operation, all the way down to the young boys whose sole job was to purchase throwaway cell phones for his operatives.

Cocaine wasn't the only cargo Felix was moving. The cash generated by drug sales—in hundred-thousand or even million-dollar bundles—also had to be collected and transported. In this activity, Felix was guided by Dedo, who had developed a system to deposit the huge sums—broken down in amounts of less than $10,000—in banks on both sides of the border. Occasionally, the American authorities intercepted a load of cocaine or money. When that happened, Dedo and the bosses in Sinaloa demanded answers from Felix, and it was his responsibility to find out whether the seizure was the result of sloppy work on the part of his men, or simply resulted from good police detection. Learning the truth sometimes required Felix to use extreme methods of interrogation and he had discovered that bringing a full-grown California rattlesnake into the room was often more effective than nearly beating a man to death. Over the years, Felix began to collect rattlers and other poisonous snakes. Once he learned about venomous lizards, he had to have one, and he asked Dedo to help him find a Motagua Valley beaded lizard, the rarest of them all.

Dedo stood in the compound under the hot early afternoon sun and watched the Cuiza, stretched out on the ground next to the cage and staring at the ugly lizard at eye-level. The boy was small and thin, but Dedo had detected an inner strength, a willfulness in him. His eyes reflected an intelligence that belied his inability to speak. "It's venomous," Dedo told the boy. "Don't try to touch it."

The Cuiza ignored him and continued to study the lizard.

Dedo nudged the boy's leg with the tip of his snakeskin boot. "Did you hear me? I said it's venomous."

"Chik, chik, chik."

"Make sure nothing happens to it, that's your job," Dedo said. "That's what I brought you here to do. And don't get too attached to it, because it's not staying for long. Do you understand?" When the Cuiza looked up, Dedo saw a flash of anger in the kid's eyes. "You're going on a boat trip," Dedo told him. "Ever been on a boat? Your lizard friend's going to California and you're going along to take care of him during the trip. Do you understand?"

Maria Gabriela came out to join the group standing in the compound. She was tall, slim, and barefoot. She wore an open blouse tied at her waist that showed the swell of her ample breasts, and white shorts that set off her long, tanned legs. Dedo's men glanced at her briefly and then averted their eyes. None of them wanted to be caught staring. It was after noon and she had just awakened. Her coal-black hair was tousled and her face was without makeup, but she was still beautiful. She sipped guanabana juice from a crystal glass, and bent to look at the caged reptile. "Oh," she exclaimed. "How awful. Who would want something like that? Is it a pet?"

"I wouldn't call it a pet," Dedo said. "This creature can live for half a century." He gazed for a moment at the lizard and then at Maria Gabriela. In fifty years this lizard would probably look the same. And Maria Gabriela? She was stunning now, but in fifty years? She would be seventy-seven. What would she look like? Dedo pushed the idea from his mind—he didn't really want to know. He turned to Luis and said, "Put the cage somewhere in the shade."

"I have a salon appointment in an hour," Maria Gabriela said.

Dedo told her, "Luis and one of the men can drive you into the city."

She drained her glass. "We're still going out tonight?"

"Yes, yes, I promised we would go," Dedo replied, sounding annoyed.

Maria Gabriela's carefree days were behind her. Once she began living with Dedo, she gave up her freedom. "Your men never leave my side," she told him. "When I go out, I feel anxious. I'm always afraid something will happen. I wish I could just go window shopping or sit outside and enjoy an espresso."

"You *should* worry," Dedo told her. "Culiacán's a dangerous place for an average woman. For a beautiful woman like you, who belongs to someone in the cartel, it can be deadly."

That was the problem. She "belonged" to Dedo. The possibility that she might be kidnapped or shot was always on her mind, and wherever Maria Gabriela went, at least two of his men trailed along to protect her. She felt like a captive behind the walls of Dedo's compound. When he travelled, which was often, she spent her days alone. She missed the working girls who were her friends and the fun they once had. Now her social circle was limited to the wives and girlfriends of the cartel bosses. "I can't stand most of them," she told Dedo.

But no matter how much she grumbled, Maria Gabriela never forgot how lucky she was. Before she met Dedo, she had worked the all-night narco parties in Culiacán, consuming whatever drugs were available and lavishing her affections on anyone who showed interest. She was invited everywhere because she was eye candy—men stared when she entered a room. Beneath her high spirits, however, Maria Gabriela was worried. The fiesta wouldn't last forever. Soon there would be younger, prettier women. Before she was thirty, she had to find a *papi rico*—a sugar daddy—to take care of her. If he loved her, all the better.

One evening, during a drug-fueled celebration at the home of one of the top Sinaloa bosses, she caught Dedo's eye, and a few days later he asked her to come to his home. In the beginning, he simply called for her once or twice a week and they spent the time making love. When they were together, he did most of the talking and she was happy to lie quietly, touching him, and listening to whatever he had to say—he knew so much about so many interesting things. Maria Gabriela particularly liked the tropical nights that followed the scorching Sinaloan summer days, when they lay naked on the lounges by his pool and stared up at the stars in the black Mexican sky.

The first time he made love to her in the shallow end, she said, "The water frightens me, I'm not a good swimmer."

He held her around the waist and said, "Don't worry, I'll teach you how to swim."

She knew Dedo was part of the cartel, and whatever he did had to be important because he lived like a king, but he never told her anything about his work and she didn't ask. There were periods when he was away and didn't call her for weeks, and he once told her that he travelled to places like New York, London, and Zurich—cities she had never seen. After one trip to Europe, he brought her a pair of diamond stud earrings and said that he had been looking at gems in Amsterdam.

Dedo was different from the other cartel men. She had never seen him use drugs, he wasn't a loudmouth, and he didn't show off. He chose not to live in Tierra Blanca, the exclusive hillside neighborhood where the top cartel bosses had their villas and mansions. Instead, he had settled outside of town, but like the others, had an enormous piece of property surrounded by high walls with closed-circuit security cameras and razor wire, and armed guards who patrolled 24 hours a day. His home was magnificent; she had never seen anything like it. The other narco residences were gaudy—painted bright colors and filled with oriental rugs, marble statues, ugly furniture, and collections of pistols and machine guns plated in gold. Dedo lived in a stark, modern house with floor to ceiling windows, white walls, and a kitchen full of gleaming stainless steel. The only decoration was the paintings hanging everywhere. When he told her the names of the artists, which he said were famous, they meant nothing to her.

She was attracted to Dedo the moment she saw him. His body was like his house—beautiful but simple. He had no tattoos, wore none of the gold chains and bracelets favored by the other narco bosses, and she loved the beautiful proportions of his physique. He was tall, with a strong upper body and shoulders from a lifetime of swimming. Unlike most Mexican men who had thick black hair, Dedo's hair was pale and he wore it cut very short. From a distance, it looked like he was bald. He also had steel gray eyes, a rarity in Mexico. Like many of the cartel bosses, he had an explosive, violent temper, but he was always gentle and soft-spoken with her.

In time, Dedo asked to see more of her, and Maria Gabriela began to spend the night at his home. Her nickname was Gabi, but he chose to call her Maria. He would telephone, simply say, "Maria, come," and send two armed men to pick her up in his silver Mercedes. He always paid her well, very well. When he finally told her, "Stop screwing other men," and asked her to live with him, Maria Gabriela thought she had accomplished her goal—she had found a wealthy, powerful man to take care of her.

Dedo was a good lover and Maria Gabriela was certain he cared for her and would never mistreat her, but she worried that there was a gulf between them she could never surmount. Sometimes at the peak of their lovemaking, when another man would be gasping, groaning, and whispering words of adoration, Dedo would be silent, gazing at her with a distant look in his gray eyes. As time passed, she began to wonder how long her sexual hold on him would last.

Almost two years after she began living with Dedo, Maria Gabriela told him about the Cuiza. "There's a young boy," she said. "His real name is Jorge, but everyone calls him the *La Cuiza*—the Little Gecko— because he collects lizards."

They were sitting out by the pool, and Dedo was reading the *Wall Street Journal*.

"His mother Luisa was my friend, a working girl like me. No one is certain, but a *putero*—one of her customers—probably beat her to death." Maria Gabriela thought of her friend from long ago—it was too late to do anything for Luisa now, but perhaps she could help her young son. "Jorge was only five at the time, and after Luisa was killed, he had no one. We took turns, caring for him for a few days or weeks, but that was all anyone could do. No one had the time to raise a child. He has never had a real home and now that he's older, he just drifts from place to place, sleeping in someone's entryway or kitchen, eating meals wherever he finds them. He's been living in a woman's garage but she's moving to Guadalajara with her boyfriend."

"What about his father?"

Maria Gabriela shrugged. "*Quien sabe?*"

"So why are you telling me all this?" Dedo had asked, without looking up from his newspaper.

"He's still just a child and he needs a home. Sometimes he even lives on the street."

"Plenty of kids live on the streets."

"There's something else. He doesn't talk. He stopped speaking after his mother died and that's why he never told anyone exactly what happened to her. He's a little strange—he collects lizards and walks around imitating gecko sounds." Maria Gabriela took Dedo's hand and pulled away the newspaper. "Could he live here?" she pleaded. "I feel so sorry for him. He won't survive on the street."

"He doesn't talk, and he makes lizard noises? Are you serious?"

"Yes, but he can hear, and if you tell him something, he understands. Actually, he's very smart. Maybe he could help clean the house, or take care of the pool."

"I have people who do that."

"It would be good, wouldn't it, to have someone around who can't talk?" She forced a small smile, hoping he would find her joke funny.

Dedo didn't smile. "No, it wouldn't. The last thing I need around here is a kid who makes lizard sounds." He picked up the *Wall Street Journal* and continued reading.

Maria Gabriela was disappointed, but didn't mention the Cuiza again. Months later, Dedo surprised her by asking, "That kid, the one who collects lizards, what happened to him?"

"He's still around," she said. "The last I heard, he was working as a lookout at a *tiendita*—a little drug shop."

"Bring him over. I have a job for him."

The Cuiza was wild with excitement as he followed Luis to the back of the house. He couldn't take his eyes off the cage containing the miraculous black creature with the bumpy skin and the yellow patches on its body. It was *un gigante*, so much larger than any lizard he had ever seen. Mexico was swarming with common geckos that scurried across the walls and ceiling at night, eating bugs and chirping to each other. He had captured hundreds of them. He kept them in boxes, talked to them, tried to play with them, and finally, if they survived the ritual, he set the little reptiles free. He had also collected a few very special green and blue lizards, and even a couple of spiky Mexican Horned Lizards, that squirted blood from their eyes, but never anything that compared to this lizard. In the cage, the Cuiza saw the most beautiful creature on the face of the earth. He saw a true Lizard King.

Luis placed the cage in the shade behind the house, on the small cement pad that surrounded the steel doors embedded in the earth. The boy was not allowed in this spot, but today he ignored the rules—as soon as Luis left, the Cuiza lay down beside the cage and stared at the creature resting on top of the moss and wood chips. It had delicate feet with long thin claw-toes that looked like miniature fingers. Its pink tongue never stopped flicking in and out of its wide mouth. The Cuiza tried to get as close as possible to the remarkable creature. He pressed his face up against the cage and watched the lizard's pulse rise and fall in the skin on the side of its neck.

The black tail, with yellow rings around it, was thick and heavy. Did this Lizard King possess the defense mechanism that the smaller lizards had, which allowed them to shed their tails to distract predators? How many times had the Cuiza held one of his small geckos up by its tail, only to end up with just the twitching appendage between his fingers while the lizard itself fell to the ground and skittered away? How often had he watched a separated tail twist and jump around, as if it had a mind of its own? The Cuiza had turned the tail-separation into a ritual, and he never allowed a gecko to go free until he forced it to release its tail. He never tired of the ceremony, no matter how many times he went through it, because it reminded him of his mother. The Cuiza studied the strong, thick tail of the creature and decided that this Lizard King would never have to lose its tail to escape from a predator—he *was* the predator!

The reptile began to scratch at the moss in the cage, and stared at the Cuiza with black eyes.

The Cuiza met the lizard's gaze and sensed a message: *todo va bien.* The Cuiza trembled with excitement. The soft, dreamlike voice of the

Lizard King told him that everything would be all right. The Cuiza had so many questions to ask, and in return he had secrets to share—things he would never reveal to the common geckos he collected. He whispered, "Chik, chik, chik." He wanted to be closer to the Lizard King.

The lizard continued to stare. Its pink tongue beckoned him.

What? the Cuiza thought. *What are you saying?*

The lizard moved its tail.

I can touch you? The Cuiza unlatched the gate on the front of the cage. *You will let me touch you?*

The lizard stared.

The Cuiza opened the gate, put his hand inside the cage, and tentatively caressed the lizard's head with his fingertips. The lizard's bumpy skin felt as hard as steel. The Cuiza moved his fingers over the lizard's back and felt a warm feeling. It started in his fingertips and travelled up his arm. The heat increased and spread throughout his body. The Cuiza had never felt such a sensation—it was more than warmth, it was a glow he felt throughout his body. A radiance, a sense of well-being, was coming to him from the Lizard King.

With clumsy strokes of its front legs, the lizard began to burrow into the wood chips and the Cuiza moved his hand away from the reptile's back. *Stay,* the Cuiza thought. *I am your friend. Don't hide from me.* He wondered if the lizard was hungry. *Do you want something to eat? Crickets, or bird's eggs? What do you eat? Please stay.*

The lizard continued to burrow.

When we are better friends, will you share your secrets? Where do you come from? How long have you lived? Have you fought other lizards? Tell me, the Cuiza pleaded silently. *Tell me, and I'll tell you the story about the little gecko, and my mother, and the man who killed her.*

The heat of the day began to subside and the Cuiza felt a faint breeze. The Lizard King had burrowed under the wood chips and disappeared.

Dedo appeared at the back of the house and saw the Cuiza lying on the ground next to the cage. The boy was small for his age—Maria Gabriela said he was eleven—and painfully thin. He was shy and never made eye contact, which was something Dedo didn't like.

The Cuiza looked up when he heard Dedo approach. "Chik, chik, chik."

Dedo grabbed the boy by the arm and yanked him to his feet. "Move," he growled. "How many times have I told you to stay away from here? Take the damn cage somewhere else. And keep quiet. I'm tired of listening to your strange sounds. Do you understand?" At that moment, Dedo decided to get rid of the Cuiza and his geckos away as soon as he delivered the lizard to Felix.

The Cuiza was not stupid and had seen many things since he had arrived. Even though he was not supposed to ever go to the back of the house, he knew what went on there. He had watched the steel doors swing open, revealing the stairway leading down into the earth. He had seen the men arrive in pickup trucks and shiny Cadillac Escalades, and watched them descend the steps, dragging large duffel bags and enormous suitcases behind them. Later, when they left, he could see that the suitcases and duffels were empty. The Cuiza was not stupid. He knew what the men had left behind.

He dragged the heavy cage across the grass to his tiny room at the side of the garage. He hated this harsh man Dedo, who finished every conversation with "Do you understand?" Of course he understood.

Dedo watched the kid for a moment as he struggled with the cage, and then went back into the house. He had work to finish before taking Maria Gabriela out for one of their infrequent visits to a local club. When he was in Culiacán, he spent most of his time secluded behind the high walls of his home or conferring with the other cartel bosses. He had no reason to go into the city—he valued his privacy and Culiacán was a dangerous place. Dedo had a satellite dish and a fully outfitted electronic office that allowed him to track financial events and monitor markets throughout the world. He also had a screening room, and sometimes he and Maria Gabriela sat alone in his private theater and watched new releases of Mexican and Spanish films. Dedo actually preferred American films, but her English was limited and the only U.S. films they did watch were poorly dubbed in Spanish.

He had a full-time cook and they ate most of their meals inside his compound. On the infrequent occasions when they did go out, as they planned to do this evening, Dedo was careful not to follow a routine. For his safety, he kept a low profile and tried to stay out of sight, and didn't even live in Tierra Blanca with the other bosses. His objective was to remain as anonymous as possible. He detested publicity or notoriety of any kind and made a point of living in the background. Once, when he left a small, unknown restaurant in Mexico City with Susana Manterola, a Brazilian movie star, a photographer took their picture. When it appeared in a newspaper the next morning, Dedo was furious and ordered one of his men to kill the photographer. While many of the drug bosses reveled in the popular *narcocorridos*—drug ballads—written about their exploits and sung by prominent Mexican singers like El Grupo Cartel, Dedo was quick to say, "I don't want anyone singing about me with guitars and trumpets. No one should care about who I am or what I'm doing." There were cartel men who fueled their public image and posed for pictures and YouTube videos with their exotic pets and expensive automobiles, but Dedo thought they were inviting trouble. His greatest fear was a bullet in the head from an assassin at a stoplight. For that reason, all of his vehicles had tinted, bulletproof glass, and the windows were never lowered.

The austerity of Dedo's life in Culiacán was offset by the frequent and lavish trips he made to financial capitals around the world in his quest to invest the cartel's money. While he travelled, Maria Gabriela remained in Culiacán behind the walled fortress that was his house and she was clearly getting restless. She had little to do while he was away, and even when he was home, he was often busy and unavailable to be with her. Recently he had considered ending their liaison and sending her away. Dedo was reluctant to admit it, but her attraction was beginning to fade. She was beautiful and sensual—a tall, voluptuous Mexican beauty with coal black hair and dark eyes—but Dedo was losing interest and longed for the more sophisticated women he knew. Their age difference—at forty-two, he was fifteen years older—wasn't as significant as her lack of education. Other than sex, they had little in common and had long since run out of things to talk about. Her life experience was limited and the financial world he lived in was a complete mystery to her.

What to do about Maria Gabriela was complicated by the fact that she had lived with Dedo for almost three years. He had originally supposed that when the time came, he would give her a large sum of money and buy her an apartment in Colinas de San Miguel, the part of town where narco gang members lived. Unfortunately, now it wasn't that simple. Once she was removed from his protection, she could be taken in a moment and forced, even tortured, to give up information and details about him that he worked so hard to conceal. She knew his personal habits, not to mention the layout of his entire property. Once, in a total lapse of judgment, Dedo had even taken her down the stairs into the vault. Foolishly, he had hoped to act out a fantasy—making love on a bed of millions of dollars. As it turned out, the money wasn't the aphrodisiac he had imagined. When they entered the vault, the sight of all the cash had a glacial effect on Maria Gabriela. She stood immobile, like an ice statue, until Dedo led her back up the stairs and sealed the vault. He had made a serious mistake that night—a mistake which had determined Maria Gabriela's fate. It was just a matter of time. He knew what he had to do, but hadn't decided how to do it.

Maria Gabriela had begged to go to one of her favorite places, the Penthouse Klub, an exclusive spot packed with the beautiful people from Culiacán. She loved the light show, the music, and the excitement of the crowd. The problem was that Dedo only took her there when the other narco bosses attended. On those nights, the *Culiche*—the natives of Culiacán—were denied entrance and the Klub was filled only with cartel men, their women, and their security guards. This was a great disappointment to Maria Gabriela, because she wanted to be with the *Culiche*, not the drug-lords. Against his better judgment, Dedo had agreed to take her there on a night when no one from the cartel would be in attendance.

They stayed at the Klub until after 1:00 a.m. Dedo was uncomfortable the entire time and regretted the outing. He was angry with himself. Violating his personal safety rules was a good way to be killed. When Maria Gabriela asked him to dance, he refused, and spent the evening sitting with his guards at a table in the shadows. While she moved around the club talking to acquaintances, Dedo scanned the room and imagined what he would do if a gun battle erupted. Maria Gabriela managed to enjoy herself that evening, but Dedo spent it thinking about the night members of La Familia killed five people outside a club in Michoacan and rolled their severed heads out onto the dance floor.

When they returned home, Maria Gabriela was tired and slightly drunk and went directly upstairs to bed. Dedo lingered in the living room. He poured himself a large shot of brandy, sipped the rich brown liquid, and felt the alcohol burn in his throat. He paced the antique hardwood floor and thought about tomorrow's boat trip.

"You can't just throw it in the back of a pickup and send it up here," Felix had told Dedo when they discussed getting the lizard to Los Angeles. "They'll confiscate it at the border. How about delivering it to Catalina Island on your new boat? I know a spot on the leeward side where I could come out and pick it up."

"That's a good idea," Dedo had replied. "Let me talk to my captain." His new $23 million yacht, the *Exchange Rate*, had been tied up at a marina in Mazatlan since he purchased it four months ago and this would be a chance to log some hours on the engines. He had never had much of an interest in boats, but the *Exchange Rate* was special, it was a work of art. A famous marine architect had designed it and each of the three decks was beautifully appointed. Below, in the engine room, each of the twin V-16 marine diesels generated 3,600 horsepower and the 34-knot cruising speed was faster than anything close to its size. It had been an impulse purchase—Dedo was normally a careful buyer, but as soon as he saw the pictures, he had to have it.

His captain, an Australian named Mason, had told him a rendezvous off Catalina Island, near Los Angeles, would be easy. "It's about 1,000 nautical miles each way. If we don't make any stops and the weather's clear, the round-trip will take about a week. We'll be running against the wind and current on the trip north, but it'll be faster on the way back. If we go, we'll need a chef. Should I hire one?"

Dedo had given the captain permission to engage a chef and then called Felix. "Okay," he told him. "I'll send the lizard on my boat. I'll call you as soon as I have it here in Culiacán." Afterward, Dedo had asked Maria Gabriela if she would enjoy making the trip to California with the Cuiza and the lizard. "Invite a few friends," he told her. "You can relax, have some fun, and not have to worry about your safety."

Maria Gabriela was thrilled, and had asked three friends to join her. "It's a luxury yacht," she told them. "Dedo says its 37 meters long. Do you have any idea how big that is? We'll have it all to ourselves for a week. *Sera una gran pachanga*—we'll have a ball."

Dedo had been pleased when she said she would go.

He drank another brandy and glanced at his watch—it was after 2:00 a.m. Dedo turned off the lights in the living room, and by the time he reached the top of the stairs, he had made up his mind. When he entered the dark bedroom, he heard Maria Gabriela's soft breathing. Dedo undressed, dropped his clothes on the floor, and crept into bed. He pulled her to him, and she responded, pressing her warm, damp body against him. They made love quickly and she uttered little sighs of pleasure, but remained half-asleep.

Afterward, Dedo rolled onto his back, on top of the sheets. He stared at the red digital clock and watched the minutes pass. It was a night when he would not sleep at all. Finally, he leaned over, inhaled the fragrance of Maria Gabriela's skin and brushed his lips across her bare shoulder. "*Hasta luego, Maria,*" he whispered before he stepped naked onto the cool tile floor and went downstairs into his office.

The computer monitors cast a blue-green glow in the room and Dedo sat down at his desk without turning on the light. He stared at the colored bands of the time-zone map that tracked the hours of the key financial markets across the world. In Culiacán, it was 2:35 a.m. on a Monday morning. His eye followed the colored sectors east across the International Date Line, where it was Tuesday afternoon in China and other parts of Asia and the financial markets in Shanghai and Tokyo had already closed. His gaze travelled on toward Europe, stopping in Frankfurt where it was Monday morning and the market had just opened. Moving on to London, it was an hour earlier and the stock exchange there wouldn't open for another half hour. Closer to home, in the Americas, the Bovespa in Sao Paolo wasn't even stirring, Wall Street was deep asleep, and the Bolsa Mexicana in Mexico City wouldn't begin trading for more than six hours. Dedo glanced at the monitor with the international financial news feed for a moment and then turned to look at the 24-hour Forex—foreign currency exchange—screen. In Mexico, the dollar was trading at 13.38 pesos.

Now wide-awake, Dedo was again preoccupied with his number one problem—money. From his computer, he activated the steel doors at the back of the house and by the time he walked around from his office, still naked, the doors were open and the stairway was illuminated. He descended to the entry of the vault, where he entered a set of numbers into the locking system and placed his palm on a sensor plate. When the heavy security door swung open, he caught the usual whiff of the stale air inside. Paper money, especially large amounts of it, had a peculiar smell. He regretted the fact that there was no ventilation system for this vault, which was really just a huge titanium-steel box set underground and surrounded by concrete walls.

In the anteroom, cash was scattered all over the floor. This was the shipment that had been delivered just before Luis arrived with the lizard. Following procedure, the men had unloaded the money and departed. Dedo reserved the responsibility of counting the rolls of $100 bills himself. It was something he did after every delivery unless he was travelling. He also ran random packets through the bill-counter, making sure that each totaled precisely $10,000.

Dedo and the bosses had initially argued about whether it would be advisable to let a few $100 bills "disappear" from time to time. After all, some of them argued, did it matter? The cartel had billions of dollars. What was $100 here or there? Perhaps allowing a little pilferage would forestall some men from deciding to strike out on their own and go into competition. Dedo was absolutely against it. "If you let them steal $100," he said, "then they will take $200, or $1,000, or maybe even an entire packet. Where would it stop? How much skimming is too much?

And if they ever decide to go against us, we have to be ruthless, call in our *gavilleros*—trigger men—and put a stop to it." Ultimately, Dedo prevailed and the bosses agreed. No theft, no matter how small, would be tolerated, just as it would not be allowed in any other business. He had developed a simple system to prevent "leakage." Each packet bore a number that identified the source of the money, and every person in the chain of transfer of that packet was individually accountable for the amount being correct. If Dedo found it was short, everyone in the group was killed, no matter who was actually responsible for the theft. It was an unforgiving system and there were no exceptions. It worked—after the first deaths, there were no more shortfalls.

Dedo stepped over the money and walked into the main part of the vault. In the flickering glare of the harsh fluorescent lights, he stared at his problem—the mountain of neatly stacked bundles, each totaling $10,000. These were not the bank-bricks of new hundred dollar bills with U.S. Treasury money bands still on them. This was money with blood on it—soiled, crumpled, and worn. He had once calculated that as many as 150,000 people worked for the Sinaloa Cartel alone, and its annual revenues exceeded $2 billion. Of course there were expenses—everyone had to be paid—but each year almost $1.5 billion constituted what economics textbooks called "free cash flow." More money arrived almost every day from shipments across the border, from collections in Mexico, Central and South America, and from around the world. The drug trade was a multinational business that generated a tsunami of cash. The flow was relentless and there was no end in sight. The most recent count in Dedo's vault alone was $2,495,750,000, and this was not the only place the Sinaloa Cartel's money was stored. Dedo's problem, his continuing nightmare, was the fact that they were drowning in $100 bills and the cash was coming in much faster than he could launder and invest it. Every day, sometimes several times a day, Dedo thought about his battle with the money. It was nerve-wracking, and it weighed heavily on him, but he was doing what he loved.

When he graduated from the London School of Economics, Dedo took a job on a trading desk at JPMorgan in New York. For the first time, he felt the incredible adrenaline rush that came from trading billions of dollars of foreign currencies. The excitement, the sheer power of controlling mega-amounts of money soon became a drug he craved. Now he was living his dream. He was investing, or trying to invest, unimaginable amounts of money. He was addicted—not to the cartel's drugs, but to its money.

As a result of Dedo's efforts, the Sinaloans now owned hundreds of businesses—restaurants, laundries, and supermarkets—stretching across Mexico. He had also used cash to buy guns, luxurious homes, and exotic cars, but he soon found he was wasting time with such small-time purchases. While it was possible to unload a few million dollars here and there in suitcases packed with $100 bills, it wasn't feasible to deliver a truckload of cash to buy something truly big and valuable. Large sums of money had to be wire-transferred by a financial institution, and it was no longer possible to deposit cash sums over $10,000 into the banking system—the Americans had put a stop to that. Drug money had to be "laundered," that is, it had to appear to come from a lawful source, and it was Dedo's job to convert it into legitimate funds that could be deposited in a bank and then used to purchase high-value assets. He was making progress—he had recently spent millions on large amounts of sparsely populated real estate in Honduras to use as growing and warehousing facilities. He had also acquired an office building and hotel in Hong Kong, a string of villas on the Cote d'Azure, and a cement factory in Indonesia. The investment of which he was most proud, however, was the one that allowed the Sinaloans to surpass the godfather of the Juarez Cartel. In an earlier generation, Amadeo Carrillo Fuentes had been called the Lord of the Skies because he owned a private fleet of 727 aircraft. Dedo had outdone Fuentes when he purchased a much larger fleet of 737 passenger jets, and then leased them to a budget air carrier in Brazil.

Dedo was always exploring new money-laundering alternatives, which kept him on the move around the world. He had an upcoming meeting in Berlin with a Russian group that claimed it could sanitize large amounts of drug money through the Eastern European banking system. Dedo was dubious and didn't trust the *Rusas*, but decided to meet them anyway—he might learn something. He was also investigating opportunities to use cash to purchase industrial and gem-quality diamonds, as well as fine art, and this offered promise. Finally, he was considering an entry into the fish business in South America. He had discovered that commercial fishing fleets throughout the region were paid in cash, and he planned to purchase the catch with drug money and then sell the fish on the open market

Dedo stared again at the wall of money in the vault. The sight of all the cash, and the realization that more would soon be arriving, was depressing and not something he wanted to think about in the early hours of this morning. He would go for a swim. He closed the vault and outer doors, walked around the house and stretched out on one of the pool lounges to wait for the first golden rays of the morning sun. The moment just before sunrise was the perfect time to admire the view. A city of hills, Culiacán was located between the rugged Sierra Madres and the lush green agricultural flatland that ran west to the Pacific Ocean. At this hour, before its 700,000 inhabitants awoke, it was peaceful and quiet, and the air was clear.

In the harsh light of day however, Culiacán wasn't just any city—it was the capital of Sinaloa and the center of the Mexican drug trade. Sure, it had the typical neighborhoods with vacant lots full of weeds, half-finished homes with piles of construction debris, and streets strewn with broken-down cars and bags of garbage, but unlike other Mexican cities, Culiacán thrived on a narco-culture of money and its citizens flaunted their wealth. The affluence, the opulence, was plain to see in the elegant neighborhoods, the boulevards jammed with exotic cars, and the streets lined with expensive shops and restaurants. Culiacán was a city of opportunity. A young boy could start his first job as a lookout guarding a little drug shop, move on to transporting bags of marijuana and cocaine, and as a teenager, graduate to the big job of killing people. Every kid who started work for the cartel received a cell phone. Soon he might have several, and even earn enough to buy a game console. Eventually, he could buy a high-tech Japanese bike and ride through the city showing off his tattoos and wearing half-a-dozen solid gold rosaries. If he lived long enough, and was clever enough, he might even ascend into the narco hierarchy and begin to dream of real wealth.

In the nine years since Dedo had arrived, the city had undergone a drastic change. The Sinaloa Cartel was the largest and most powerful of the drug empires, but shifting alliances and divisions within the ranks had given rise to a brutal turf war that had spread across Mexico and was consuming Culiacán. The Juarez Cartel, Los Zetas, La Familia Michoacana, and the Gulf Cartel, were each trying to wrest territory and influence from the Sinaloans—as well as fighting with each other. The American "war on drugs," which had been going on for twenty years, was a joke, a nuisance compared to the internal war among the narco bosses vying for control.

Beneath the energy and excitement of the city, fear of violence suffused every aspect of daily life. Survival meant being attentive. It didn't matter if you were a boss, a cartel foot soldier, or just an innocent bystander—everyone scanned the streets for impending violence. Street battles with heavy-caliber weapons and rocket-propelled grenades were common and bodies riddled with lead were left where they fell on the pavement. The violence was so overwhelming that Dedo had begun to wonder whether the ambushes, massacres, kidnappings, and torture could get any worse. When he heard that some assassins were dissolving their victims in barrels of acid, he felt things had reached a new low.

For his own part, Dedo avoided most parts of the city, never walked on the street, and when he did get out of his car, his men, wearing Kevlar vests, surrounded him. Years earlier, he had purchased a large piece of land in one of Culiacán's poorest neighborhoods and built a recreational area and a swimming pool. At first, he had visited the park often, and spoke to some of the families enjoying the facility. That seemed like another lifetime—now it was much too dangerous to go out in a public area like that, even with his bodyguards, and it had been years since he had visited the pool. Although Dedo continued to fund its upkeep, he avoided the park.

Dedo was one of the few outsiders at the top of the cartel hierarchy. He came from a different background than most of the drug lords, who had grown up in poor towns in the Sierra Madres where people suffered a hard existence living in hovels made of cinderblocks. Dedo had no poverty to escape. He grew up in Mexico City and lived a blessed childhood. His father owned a small Mexican chemical business that grew large when it began to supply the Cartels with the ingredients used to make methamphetamine. His mother was Swiss, and had worked for a chemical company in Basle when she met his father. Dedo inherited his intellect and business sense from his father. His grey eyes came from his mother.

When his father brought him to the State of Sinaloa for the first time, Dedo stood in the dust and blasting heat and felt the moisture evaporating from his skin. "Those mountain highlands," his father had told him, pointing off into the distance, "are ideal for growing poppies. All they need is sunlight and moisture." Then he turned and pointed in the direction of the Pacific Ocean, and continued, "And out in those valleys between the mountains and the coast, the climate is perfect for growing marijuana." Finally, his father looked at Dedo and told him, "Fortunately for us, sunshine and water don't produce methamphetamine. For that, they need chemicals—a lot of chemicals—and that's why we're here."

After his father's death, Dedo's mother returned to Switzerland, where the profits from the family chemical business had been accumulating for years. By that time, Dedo was already working for the Sinaloans. When she passed, Dedo inherited the small family fortune, but he had already amassed much greater wealth of his own.

Dedo watched the orange rim of the sun appear over the jagged edges of the Sierra Madres, sending light into the sky above Culiacán. It was time to clear his mind. He walked to the edge of the pool, did a series of stretches, and dove in. The water was cool and invigorating. As he began his vigorous workout, Dedo's mind was on his upcoming trip to Berlin. He would fly via London. There was a woman, Fiona, a painter who lived in Knightsbridge. He decided to call her.

The Cuiza was crouched down behind the stone wall at the back of the garage when he heard the splash from the pool. An hour ago, he had left the Lizard King outside the tiny room where he slept, and had crept down to peer through a window into the bedroom where Luis was making the two-backed animal, lying belly to belly with one of the young maids. When their lovemaking approached a climax, the Cuiza opened the box containing a small gecko.

Six years had passed and the details of his mother's face were beginning to blur in his memory, but he could recall every detail of the night she died. He also remembered the tattoo—a skull surrounded by barbed wire—inked on the back of the neck of the man who killed her.

"*Puta.*"

When the man spoke, Jorge had edged farther under the bed.

The room was filled with the lemon scent his *mamá* wore when she worked, and the odor of rancid sweat from the naked body grinding away on top of her. The man, who had come many times to visit his mother, intensified his efforts. The bed shook and the sagging web of springs holding the filthy mattress pressed down on top of Jorge. In a few months, he would be six—too big to crawl under his mother's bed.

A cuiza, a small, unremarkable gray-green gecko, crawled through the dust on the concrete floor under the bed, trapped between Jorge and the wall.

"No, dammit, no, no," the man bellowed. The bed stopped swaying.

Jorge heard the sound of a hand slapping flesh and his *mamá* whimpered.

"You pig," the man said. "Do better than that. Damn you."

The second impact was louder, harder. Jorge heard her high-pitched cry. He reached for the gecko and it flattened itself against the concrete, remaining motionless in the dust. Its head was inches from Jorge's face. He looked at its black eyes and it stared back. A live insect—a tiny fly— struggled in its jaws. The little lizard swallowed the insect.

The man became furious and the blows were more powerful. This had happened before, but it had never gone on so long or sounded so brutal. His mother's cries turned to screams and Jorge tried not to listen. He grabbed the cuiza's tail with his fingers.

The gecko made a chirping sound—*chik, chik, chik*—shed its tail, and skittered away.

The force of the final blow knocked his *mamá* off the bed. From his hiding place, Jorge saw the brown skin of her naked back as she lay on the floor. He watched the man's bare foot poke her and then push her body aside before he walked out the room. When Jorge crawled out from under the bed, he saw the blood dripping from his mother's face, collecting in a small red pool on the floor. He wanted to wake her, but his brain no longer controlled his voice. His throat was frozen—no words came. Jorge lay down on the floor, curled up next to his *mamá*, and cried silent tears. Above him, he saw the tailless gecko climbing the bedroom wall.

Just as Luis and the young maid reached the final spasm of their lovemaking, the Cuiza took the small gecko out of the box. He thought of the night under his mother's bed, watched the man and woman lying naked on the mattress, and held the reptile up by its tail. It struggled for a moment, emitting soft chirps—*chik, chik, chik*—before it detached from its tail, fell to the ground, and disappeared across the cement into the vegetation.

"Are you ready to go?" was the first thing Dedo said when he called. "Is everything set?"

"Yessir, Mr. Delgado, we're all set, the boat's spic and span," Mason said. They were not ready to go—one of the eight crew members had been shacked up with his girlfriend for two days, and Mason had no idea where to find him—but that was not something to tell the new owner, the man who was now signing the checks. "Will you be making the trip with us?" Mason asked.

"Me? No, but you'll have six passengers. Four women, one of my men, and a kid. One of the women, her name is Maria Gabriela, is my...uh... girlfriend. She's in charge. It's just a quick round trip. You're delivering something to Catalina, and then coming right back."

"Delivering something? Yessir." Mason's imagination went to work.

"A lizard."

"A lizard? Sir?"

"That's what I said, a lizard. You know, a reptile. In a cage. The kid's job is to take care of the lizard during the trip. Nothing must happen to it—it's very rare. When you get to Catalina, you're going to drop the kid and the lizard at a spot called Paradise Cove, it's supposed to be the leeward side of the island. I'm sure it's on your charts."

"Deliver a lizard and a kid. On the leeward side of Catalina. Yessir."

"After you drop them off, a 36-foot Bertram called *Truckin* will come in and pick up the lizard. Once the Bertram's gone, you go back, get the kid, and then bring everyone home. Got that?"

"Yessir."

"The night before you get to Catalina, call the captain of the Bertram. His number in California is 310-317-4545. He'll give you specific instructions and you do whatever he says. Any questions?"

"No sir."

"Good. Come up to Altata tomorrow. I'll send everyone out on a launch at 11:00 a.m. If you need me during the trip, call me on the satellite phone."

"Yessir. Eleven in the morning."

Mason had mixed feelings when he hung up. The good news was that they would finally be taking the *Exchange Rate* out to sea. He and the crew had spent the last four months on the boat in a marina in Mazatlan. Living in port on a $23 million boat wasn't so bad, but it was like owning a Ferrari and sitting in it in the garage. Mason was a yacht captain, not a houseboat sitter. His place was out on the water, where he could crank up the bloody engines and feel the sea spray on his face.

A Chilean billionaire, a fat-ass who had made his money mining copper and tin, had built the boat and named it *Penique de Cobre*—the *Copper Penny*. Mason, an Aussie who liked to drink, had captained it for two years until the mining magnate had a heart attack and died in his sleep while on a cruise. His wife, whose feet had never even touched the deck, immediately fired her husband's onboard "massage therapist" and put the *Penique* up for sale. A few weeks later, someone expressed interest and sent a naval engineer to the Yacht Club de Chile to look at the boat. Mason was stunned when the man, Pella Delgado, wrote a check for the yacht twenty-four hours later and hired him and the rest of the crew, sight unseen. When Delgado registered the boat in the Cayman Islands as the *Exchange Rate*, Mason saw that his address was listed as Basle, Switzerland. Three months later, he finally appeared and spent a day on the boat. He spoke English with a Mexican accent, and Mason was certain he was involved with one of the drug cartels.

Now, the day before they planned to go to sea, Mason was uneasy as he sat in the wheelhouse mapping the waypoints for the trip to Catalina and programming coordinates into the GPS. "What do you think?" he asked his first mate. "The guy sends his engineer to check out the boat and the next day spends $23 million to buy it. Then he doesn't even come to look at it for three months. Who does something like that?" Mason didn't wait for the first mate to answer. "Someone who has so much bloody money he doesn't know what to do with it. Like a cartel boss." Mason turned the pages in the chart book and continued, "Are we really supposed to believe we're going to all the way to Catalina Island to deliver a bloody lizard?"

"What if we're carrying a shipment of marijuana or cocaine and the Coast Guard stops us?" the first mate said.

"Forget the bloody Coast Guard," Mason said. "What if we get stopped by the Mexican Navy?" Once, he'd spent a week in a Mexican jail, and that was enough.

At 11:00 a.m. the following day, the *Exchange Rate* lay at anchor in a calm sea across the bay from the town of Nuevo Altata, a beach resort west of Culiacán. In the twenty-four hours since Delgado called, Mason and the crew—minus one member—had stocked the boat with food and drink and labored furiously to make every surface sparkle. In the years he had been working on luxury yachts, first as a crewmember, then a first mate, and finally as a captain, Mason had never seen a more elegant boat than the *Penique*, or the *Exchange Rate*, as it was now called. The forward crew cabins and mess were nicer than the owner's accommodations on most yachts, and its three decks had every amenity. The fly bridge had a Jacuzzi and a sundeck. The main deck had two indoor salons, a dining room, and a galley that belonged in a gourmet restaurant. The lower deck had a master stateroom with a marble bathroom and four guest cabins. The furniture throughout was custom-made from the finest teak. There were large-screen televisions everywhere and a stereo sound system throughout the boat. Best of all, the wheelhouse had state of the art navigation and communication equipment. The controls were a captain's dream.

When the launch approached, the first mate remained on the bridge while Mason and the other crew members, all in clean, pressed white uniforms, gathered on the hydraulic swim and loading platform on the starboard side to welcome the guests.

"Holy shit," Mason heard the steward whisper when the first passenger stepped out of the launch onto the swim platform.

Mason was transfixed as well, but tried not to stare. Four of the most gorgeous women he had ever seen, wearing halter-tops and the shortest of shorts, were boarding the *Exchange Rate*. Each was more beautiful than the next. They were true Latina beauties, with tawny skin, thick manes of black hair, and figures to die for, punctuated by long shapely legs. After the women came aboard, a ragged young boy—Mason had seen kids like him doing odd jobs on docks all over the world—jumped onto the swim platform from the launch. Mason wondered who he was, then remembered Mr. Delgado had mentioned a boy who was tending to the lizard. The last passenger was a short, thick man with muscular arms and a neck as wide as his head. His skin was the dark color of old leather and he had an ugly scar that ran along the line of his jaw. While the launch crew transferred a considerable amount of luggage, he stood apart from the women and studied the yacht. The last thing to come aboard was a wire cage filled with wood chips and moss. As soon as someone from the launch placed it on the swim deck, the boy crouched down next to it and began to make strange sounds.

"Welcome aboard," Mason said, trying to ignore the kid's odd behavior. "Is that it? Do we have everything?" Mason half-expected a load of drugs to appear from the launch.

"That's all," one of the women said, and stepped forward. "I'm Maria Gabriela." She reached out to shake his hand.

"Yes Ma'am," Mason said, almost trembling when he touched her. "I'm captain Mason, and this is David, the steward. He'll show you to your cabins." Mason pointed to the kid. "Where should he stay?"

"That's the Cuiza. He stays with the lizard. Is there a place with the crew?"

The boy made more strange sounds.

"Yes, of course," Mason said.

"And this is Diego," she said, glancing at the brawny man sent to accompany them. "He has to have his own room."

"Cabin," Mason corrected her, smiling. He looked at Diego. The man looked like trouble, and Mason decided it would be best to have him somewhere where they could keep an eye on him. That meant not in the bowels of the boat. "You can have the first mate's cabin," he said to Diego, who stared back, but said nothing and didn't smile. "Well then," Mason continued, "you ladies go ahead and get settled while we get underway. We'll serve drinks and lunch on the fly bridge in half an hour." Fearful that he was gaping at the cleavage of Maria Gabriela's breasts, Mason averted his gaze and climbed the stairs to the main deck. Before he reached the bridge, he felt the vibration in the soles of his feet and heard the muffled sound of the powerful marine engines as they came to life. The *Exchange Rate* thrust its bow up and began to pick up speed.

"Wait until you see the women," Mason told the first mate when he entered the wheelhouse and took charge. "They're bloody magnificent. And it appears that Mr. Delgado sent an enforcer along."

"An enforcer?" the first mate said.

"The guy looks like a gorilla, and my guess is that he's armed. He has to have his own cabin, so I gave him yours." Before the first mate could protest, Mason said, "I want to keep an eye on him so you'll just have to bunk with me." He slid into the captain's chair and glanced at the radar and weather monitors. "Looks like clear weather."

"What about the lizard?" the first mate asked. "Did you see it?"

"They brought a cage onboard," Mason said. "But I couldn't see what was in it. The kid who's taking care of it looks like he's been living on the street. He's gonna stay with the creature in the forward crew cabin." Mason checked the chronometer. "We'll start six-hour bridge watches at noon. You take the first. That'll give you almost an hour to move into my cabin."

"What about drugs? Any kilos of cocaine?"

"No, but the women brought a shit-load of luggage. How much clothing do they need for a one-week boat trip?" Mason imagined them splashing in the Jacuzzi up on the fly bridge, wearing tiny bikinis, or maybe not wearing bikinis. He turned to focus on the weather monitor.

After picking up the passengers, the *Exchange* Rate headed 250 degrees West-Southwest, travelling past the entrance to the Gulf of California, the body of water separating the Baja California Peninsula from the Mexican mainland. At the tip of the Baja lay the fishing and resort city of Cabo San Lucas, which Mason knew well. Twenty-five years ago, when it was still a wide-open, almost lawless place, he had gone on a drinking binge one night at the Giggling Marlin, a popular Cabo hangout. When he staggered outside at midnight and fired a rescue flare into the air, it landed on the roof of the bar and set the building on fire. Mason was still laughing at the flames when the Municipal Police arrested him and threw him in jail. Mason stepped outside the wheelhouse and scanned the coast with his powerful marine binoculars. The city of Cabo was no longer visible, but interspersed along the rocky shore he saw the sandy white beaches that made it so popular.

When the *Exchange Rate* came around the peninsula and turned north, they passed a fleet of sport fishing boats returning after a day of searching for blue marlin.

By the next morning, things had changed aboard the *Exchange Rate*. The previous owner, the Chilean billionaire, was a dull old man. When he was at sea, he spent much of his morning sitting under an awning on the fly bridge, reading through thick eyeglasses or simply dozing. After a sedate lunch and half a glass of white wine, he would retire to the master suite, where his massage therapist did whatever it was she did before he dozed off for a few hours until dinner. After dinner, which was often finished before the sun set, the billionaire turned in and was not seen again until morning.

In contrast, the new passengers on the *Exchange Rate*—the four beauties—partied nonstop with an energy level Mason had not seen since his youth. They frolicked outside on the fly bridge, sunbathed topless on the swim platform, reveled in the salons and the dining room, and carried on in their cabins. From the bridge, he heard the constant sound of their chatter, laughter, and screams of amusement. Loud music streamed through the Bose speakers on every deck, adding to the clamor. Mason watched them eat, drink, pop pills and snort cocaine from the time they rose, late in the morning, until they passed out in the small hours of the night. Through it all, he couldn't get over their physical beauty.

While the women were everywhere on the boat, Diego the gorilla barely showed himself. He came out of the first mate's cabin at meal times, descended to the crew mess where he sat alone and shoveled down his food without speaking, and then returned to his cabin. Twice a day, he spent a few minutes walking around the decks, as though he was searching for something, then disappeared again into his cabin.

The kid, the one they called the Cuiza, was invisible. He never left the forward quarters—he stayed below and ate whatever the crew members brought him. The steward reported to Mason that there was in fact a big, ugly lizard in the cage, and that the kid spent his days hunched down next to it, making strange sounds.

Aside from the incessant activity of the women, the trip north was uneventful. The weather was clear and the *Exchange Rate* made good time. After passing the Mexican coastal waypoints of Bahia Magdalena and Turtle Bay on the second day, they entered U.S. territorial waters off the coast of San Diego. Mason spotted a Coast Guard cutter about 3000 meters off to starboard, headed in the same direction. He studied it through his glasses. It was half again as long as the *Exchange Rate* and Mason was certain it was one of the Fast Response boats used for drug and smuggling interdiction. Two hours later, at the end of his late afternoon shift, the cutter was still nearby, running a parallel course, following them north toward Catalina. When the first mate joined him in the wheelhouse for the shift change, Mason pointed out the windows and said, "We have company."

The first mate studied the cutter through the binoculars for a moment, and said, "Do you think they're going to board us?"

"I have no idea," Mason said, "but I'd better alert our passengers, just in case." When he left the wheelhouse, Mason stopped at the first mate's cabin and pounded on the door. "Hey," he shouted to Diego, "just putting you on notice, we may have a visit from the Coast Guard." He paused and listened for a response, but got none. Mason pounded on the door again. "Hello? Hey, d'you hear me?" When he again got no response, he gave up and went into the salon, where the four women were eating hors d'oeuvres and finishing a bottle of champagne.

"*Hola*, Captain," the woman named Marguerita said. She was sprawled across a couch when he entered, but jumped up, saluted, and approached him. She reached out to touch his arm, and her face was close to his when she said, "Join us for a drink?"

She was as tall as Mason, and he felt her warm breath on his cheek. The woman was dazzling, and he wanted to do much more than have a drink with her, but murmured, "No ma'am," and backed away. "We may have a visit from the U.S. Coast Guard, so if you brought anything on board that's—um—illegal, this would be the time to get rid of it."

The women burst into laughter. Marguerita went back to the couch and poured herself another glass of champagne. "*Salud*, Captain Mason," she purred.

Before he went down to the crew mess, Mason used the satellite phone to contact the owner of the Bertram fishing boat. He had been given no name, just a number to call. When a male voice answered, Mason said, "Hello, is this the owner of the *Truckin*?"

"Who's calling?" came the curt reply.

"This is Mason, the captain of the *Exchange Rate*."

"Go ahead."

"We're off San Clemente now. We're going to proceed to Catalina Island and anchor offshore overnight. We can send a Zodiac in to drop the boy and his companion anytime tomorrow morning." Mason smiled as he referred to the lizard as a 'companion.' "What time works for you?"

"Anchor off Paradise Cove at 7:30 a.m. and I'll call you. Got that?"

"Yes," Mason said, and waited for a further comment from the owner of the *Truckin*, but the man had already disconnected. Mason turned off the telephone and headed below to eat something before he went to his cabin to sleep.

Felix had done extensive research on the Motagua Valley beaded lizard and had found a reptile expert in Southern California who was acquainted with the creature. He hired the man to design and build a glass-enclosed space in his house, constructed to resemble the lizard's natural habitat. The expert had collected some native plants, specified the type of sand and dirt, and moved pieces of wood and stone around until he was satisfied with the layout. A small recirculating pool of water installed in one corner provided moisture.

Felix' research uncovered many of the myths about the beaded lizard, including the fable that foretold of adversity and death to anyone who captured it. It didn't bother him—he wasn't superstitious. Felix dismissed it as just another tale of the lizard. He had been counting the days and then the hours until he had his prized reptile. The previous night, Felix had barely slept—he tossed and turned, excited about the arrival of the lizard. Now, this morning, at anchor in the Pacific Ocean off Catalina Island, he put his excitement aside while he studied the other fishing boats. Wherever he went, Felix was always on the lookout, watching for anything unusual. His skills of covert surveillance had been honed over a decade of hiding in buildings, lurking in vehicles, and even crawling through the brush to spy on the DEA and other law enforcement agents who were trying to catch his *polleros*—his couriers—bringing drugs over the border. "You can never be too careful," he often told his seventeen-year-old son. "Always assume that someone is watching you. That way you'll never be surprised."

Felix was a wary and cautious man, a master of observation, and this guarded nature had kept him out of trouble and out of jail. Not only was he careful, Felix was modest and unpretentious, and he warned his son, "don't get caught up with the young drug dealers. Forget about the fast cars and flashy jewelry. If you flaunt your money, people will start asking questions." Neither his automobiles nor his fishing boat gave any hint of Felix' vast wealth. The 36-foot *Truckin* looked like any other scruffy, well-used fishing boat. The fact that he had installed one-way optical quality glass in the cabin windows, and the boat was filled with an array of binoculars, marine telescopes, and night vision equipment wasn't obvious to anyone looking at the boat from the water.

He had crossed the San Pedro Channel from Long Beach two hours earlier in the dark, made a quick run along the eastern coast of Catalina as far as Two Harbors, then turned back and dropped anchor off Paradise Cove at 7:15 a.m. By the time Felix arrived, the water around the cove was dotted with the usual weekday morning fishing boats angling for yellowtail, Bonita, and kelp bass. Felix watched men, boys, and even a couple of hearty women tending to their lines, wiping down decks and railings, and fiddling with their cell phones.

Felix baited a hook, played the line out into the water, and placed the rod in one of the holders. He poured himself a cup of coffee from a thermos, stood at the stern of his boat and became angry all over again with his son Daniel. In the early hour of the morning, when Felix awakened him, Daniel had rolled over in bed, groggy and hung over. He had been out partying all night, and said he was too tired to make the trip to Catalina. Felix was furious, but he didn't have time to argue with the boy, and had stormed out of the house. He could pick up the lizard by himself, and would deal with his spoiled, lazy son when he returned home.

For no good reason, Felix felt edgy as he bobbed around on his boat. He had an uneasy feeling in his gut that he was being watched, and had learned to pay attention to his instincts. Felix examined the surrounding fishing boats yet again and then turned his attention to Paradise Cove and the steep hillsides rising up around it. In another month, swimmers and water skiers would be crowding onto the gray-white quartz sand, but this morning the beach was deserted. Earlier, he had seen three scuba divers unload their equipment on the small dock, but now they were out in the water, and only their diving flag was visible.

He checked the time. It was 7:25 a.m. When he looked up, he caught sight of the *Exchange Rate* coming toward the island from the west. As the yacht approached, he saw that it was much bigger and more impressive than the pictures Dedo had sent him. It stood out like a sore thumb and in these waters, it would attract more attention than the Queen Mary. He reached for the satellite phone and called.

"This is Captain Mason."

"I have you in view," Felix said. "Go ahead with the drop. There's a small dock on the beach where you can unload it. We're not going to do a boat-to-boat transfer. After your Zodiac moves away from the dock and I can see that everything is clear, I'll come in and make the pickup. Don't return for the boy until we have left the area. Got that?"

"Yessir," Mason replied.

Felix studied the activity on the yacht's swim platform. Two crew members, in white uniforms, wrestled a black Zodiac into the water. A tall, shapely woman and a boy watched as one crew member stepped into the rubber dinghy and the other passed a metal cage to him. There it was—they were loading his prized beaded lizard. In just a few minutes, he would have it safely aboard his own boat and be headed home. Felix was filled with excitement as he watched the kid climb into the dinghy. The crewmember started the small outboard, the craft moved away from the swim platform and plowed through the water toward the cove.

It was a perfect California morning—the sky pale blue, the wind quiet, the water calm. A few gulls circled overhead, squawking and waiting for the anglers to throw something from their boats. It was a great day for fishing, and an even better day for collecting a rare Motagua Valley beaded lizard. Felix felt like a very lucky man. When the Zodiac reached the dock, he watched the crew member unload the cage. The kid jumped onto the dock and squatted next to the lizard—he didn't even look up when the Zodiac started back to the *Exchange Rate* without him.

Felix moistened his lips. "Thank you, Dedo, *mi amigo*," he whispered. "Thank you so much." Felix scanned the water again. Everything appeared normal and his apprehension faded. The *Exchange Rate* turned into the wind, waiting for the return of the Zodiac. He looked out across the water one last time and caught a brief flash of reflected light. He thought it had come from the direction of a small, neglected-looking fishing boat with an old outboard hanging off the back. Something on the boat—a piece of polished metal or glass—had caught the sunlight. Felix went into the cabin, took out his binoculars, and studied the small boat. He focused on the roly-poly man moving around in the stern of the boat. When a gust of wind blew his unzipped jacket open, Felix saw the gun on his hip. A man out fishing wearing a pistol? Felix couldn't tell what kind—maybe a Glock or a Sig Sauer, but it screamed law enforcement. Felix scrutinized the boat and noticed it wasn't carrying the usual fishing gear. Two fishing rods trailed limp lines in the water off the back of the boat, but there were no pole rigs, ice coolers, or bait buckets in sight. A cold chill ran through him. When he tried to gaze under the awning, into the open cockpit of the boat, he caught the reflected light once again. Felix re-focused his high-magnification binoculars, and was able to make out someone crouched at the back of the cockpit, leaning against the cabin door. That person was studying the beach with his own set of glasses, and as his boat bobbed in the water, the sunlight sent random reflections off the lenses.

Felix swallowed hard, forgot about his rare lizard, and went into escape mode. "We've got a problem," he said aloud. He had a habit of talking to himself in emergencies—it steadied him and kept him calm when deliberate action was needed. "Someone's doing surveillance," he mumbled. "They're watching the beach." Felix took a deep breath and felt his heart rate accelerate. "Go slow and act natural. Bring your line in, pull up the anchor, and get the hell out of here." He put down his glasses and called the *Exchange Rate*. When Captain Mason answered, Felix told him, "Something's wrong. We're under surveillance."

"Under surveillance?" the captain echoed. "Why?"

"I don't know, and there's no time to discuss it. I'm clearing out. Pick up your Zodiac and take off. Immediately. Forget the lizard and the boy and head for Mexican waters as fast as you can."

Mason was ninety minutes into his midnight to six a.m. bridge watch, trying again to make sense of the day's events and wondering if the Coast Guard boat, which had shadowed them, had anything to do with what had transpired. After they abandoned the boy and the lizard on the dock and started back toward Mexico, he called Mr. Delgado, who seemed surprised, but told him to follow the instructions from the captain of the *Truckin* and return home. The woman, Maria Gabriela, was very upset and demanded that they turn the boat around and pick up the boy. When Mason refused, she let loose a string of curses in Spanish, went to her cabin, and didn't come out. Mason wondered what would happen when they returned to Mexico. What would be the outcome of leaving the boy on the beach? It wasn't his fault, he had followed instructions, but he still worried about facing his boss. What kind of job security could he count on from a Swiss-Mexican who was probably a bloody cartel member? What if he was fired?

Mason swiveled in the captain's chair and scanned the multi-colored screens on the control panel. The *Exchange Rate* was fighting an unusual Southeasterly wind on the trip home, but was making good time, running at over twenty knots. Engine temperature, oil pressure, and RPM were all as they should be, and the television camera mounted on the ceiling above the twin turbines showed all was normal in the engine room. Lifting his gaze to the windows of the wheelhouse, he stared out into nothing. It was a cloudy night with no moon, the sea and the sky merged into a single dark shroud, and the running lights were a faint glow along the perimeter of the boat. The steady drone of the engines was like a lullaby and Mason, leaning back in the padded chair, fought the urge to fall asleep. He had spent most of his life working on boats, maintaining the demanding and unusual hours of a seafarer, but sometimes he still succumbed to the groggy feeling that accompanied a life divided into six-hour shifts. His eyelids closed for just a moment.

What was that? A faint cry? Mason was suddenly wide-awake, his heart pounding in his chest. He sat up and strained to listen. It had lasted only a second. Was it the call of a seagull? Not at 1:40 a.m. on the open ocean. It had sounded like it came from the starboard side, below the wheelhouse. Was someone down on the lower deck or on the swim platform? Mason held his breath and listened, but he heard nothing but the beating of his own heart and the rumble of the engines as the *Exchange Rate* plowed south through the water. He considered taking the high-powered halogen light out to check the decks, but decided against it. Was he dreaming? Had he really heard anything? There was no further sound. Mason studied the radar screen and waited for his heart rate to return to normal.

"Hey Mason. Wake up. Wake up."

The first mate's hand on his shoulder brought Mason back from a dream. He looked at his watch. It was 10:45 a.m. He wasn't due in the wheelhouse until noon. He sat up with a start. "What?"

"The woman," the first mate said. His eyes were wild. "She's gone."

"Which woman?

"Maria."

"What d'you mean she's gone?"

"She wasn't in her stateroom this morning. We've searched the entire boat."

"Jesus fucking Christ!" Mason jumped up and headed out of the cabin, barefoot, wearing just his undershorts. "Why didn't you wake me up sooner? Is she overboard? Did you call the bloody Mexican Navy?"

"Yes, I did," the first mate said, following him down the corridor. "They said it'll be six hours before they can send a ship and—"

"Jesus!" Mason wheeled around and slammed his fist against the teak railing. "She could drown in six hours if she hasn't already. We're what, five miles offshore, and they can't send help? Contact the Coast Guard. See if they can launch an air-sea rescue search. I've got to call Mr. Delgado." Mason climbed the stairs to the wheelhouse. He couldn't believe this was happening. If yesterday's call about leaving the kid on the beach wasn't bad enough, now he had to tell his new boss that his girlfriend was missing, that she might have fallen overboard. "Jesus bloody Christ," Mason breathed. He would be lucky if someone wasn't waiting to kill him the minute the *Exchange Rate* docked.

The call came earlier than Dedo had expected. He had figured it would be at least another hour before they discovered Maria Gabriela was missing. Mason, the captain, sounded frantic.

"Mr. Delgado, sir. We have a problem. Maria… uh… Maria Gabriela… your… uh… she's missing from the boat and—"

"Missing?" Dedo raised the pitch of his voice and tried to sound anxious. "What do you mean she's missing?"

"She must have gone overboard. We've searched the ship."

"Overboard? *Overboard*! When did it happen?"

"Not sure sir. Sometime last night."

"*Dios mio*," Dedo moaned into the phone. "Maria Gabriela." He paused for a few seconds and then said, "Excuse me Mason, hold on a moment, this is such a shock." He dropped the phone on the bed while he packed the remaining shirts in his suitcase. When he picked the phone up again, he said, "I'm sorry—this is quite a shock."

"I understand, sir."

"How did this happen? Did you hit bad weather?"

"No sir. We had a heavy sea, but nothing that would cause someone to fall overboard. We've turned back, and we're trying to plot a rescue area, but we have no idea what time she went over, and given the currents and wind, there's a lot of ocean to cover. Part of it is in U.S. waters and we're asking the Coast Guard for assistance. I told them that you would spend whatever was necessary to bring in extra aircraft. Is that correct?"

"Yes. Do everything possible," Dedo said. He looked at his watch. In less than an hour, he had to leave for the Culiacán airport to catch his private flight to London. In eighteen hours, he would be sitting down to dinner with Fiona, the painter who lived in Knightsbridge. "Whatever's necessary," he told Mason. "The cost doesn't matter. Just find Maria Gabriela." Luis entered the bedroom to take the luggage, and Dedo put a finger to his lips. "Keep me advised, Mason. And be sure you report this as soon as you return."

A broad smile appeared on Dedo's face as he hung up. He handed Luis his luggage. It was a win-win. Maria Gabriela had vanished and the strange boy had been left on Catalina Island.

IV | THE LIZARD

It is the beginning of the wet season and the Motagua Valley beaded lizard breaks through the shell of his egg in a nest built by his mother in an underground shelter. He remains underground for months with his siblings, and when they emerge, snakes and raptors attempt to eat them. If he is lucky enough to escape that fate—one of every four young lizards are devoured—and find enough food, he will quickly grow to a size at which predators can no longer threaten him.

He is a carnivorous forager who shuffles along in a slow, stop-and-go motion, flicking his thick, pink, forked tongue in the air and on the ground to investigate his surroundings and pick up chemical scents.

He devours nestling rabbits and climbs trees and vines to find baby squirrels as well as the eggs and fledglings of doves, trogans, and chachalacas. Sometimes he eats insects, and prefers beetle larvae. He is an excellent digger and makes frequent stops as he moves through sand and grass searching for buried snake and Spiny-tailed iguana eggs. When he finds an egg, he maneuvers his jaws around it and uses his tongue to push it to the back of his mouth before he crushes and swallows it.

An adult beaded lizard can consume large quantities when he does find food, and his entire seasonal intake of nutrition may consist of as few as three or four meals. If necessary, he can go several months without eating while he lives off the fat stored in his tail.

He is a stealthy creature, and spends less than 10% of his time engaged in physical activity. He is cold-blooded and cannot tolerate high temperatures. During the hot, dry season in Guatemala, he remains concealed in underground shelters that provide protection from the extreme temperature, foraging briefly in the late afternoon and evening. The beaded lizard endures extreme drought by absorbing the water carried in his bladder.

Because he is a nest predator, he has no need to poison or paralyze his prey, but he is not a good runner and there are times when he has to stand and defend himself against an aggressor. For this purpose, the Guatemalan beaded lizard carries toxic venom in his lower jaw, in glands that empty into his grooved teeth. If provoked, he will first hiss and swing his body from side to side, then bite and hang on, using his large jaw muscles to grind his teeth into the flesh of an attacker until the toxin works its way into the wound and affects the central nervous system. His venom is not deadly to humans, but can result in excruciating pain, weakness, and a rapid drop in blood pressure. Researchers are investigating several peptides found in the beaded lizard's venom that have important pharmacological applications.

V | RYAN

After a couple of hours crouched down at the back of the cockpit of the miserable little fishing boat, the electric sting of a muscle spasm seized Ryan Daniels' lower back and sent pain screaming down into his legs. He groaned, stood up, and leaned against the door of the cuddy cabin, waiting for the cramp to subside. It had been a long night.

It was already dark when they received word that the *Exchange Rate* had anchored off Catalina, and the two special agents, Ryan and his partner Victor, had rushed to the marina in San Pedro where the DEA had rented a fishing boat to use for surveillance. The two men had been working together for about six months and were an odd pair. Ryan was big and tall, a second-string college quarterback from the Midwest with a flat nose—broken by a football in the face—and skin with a pallor that refused to be tanned by the hot Southern California sun. Victor, with dark Mediterranean skin, was short and round, a second generation Greek-American whose last name no one could remember—it was Sotiropoulos. The other agents in the Los Angeles Field Division referred to them as Mutt and Jeff.

Standing on the floating dock, rising and falling with each wake from ships passing in the channel, Ryan had stared in disbelief. "That's our surveillance boat?" he said. "That's the best they could do?" In the weak light of the bulbs strung along the dock, it looked like a very small, very old boat.

"That's it." Victor said, bending down to take a closer look. "A 1959 Glasspar."

"What kind of engine is that? It looks ancient."

"It's an old Evinrude, a one-fifty."

"Couldn't they have rented a bigger boat? Can this thing even get us to Catalina?"

Victor pulled back the tarp, jumped aboard, and stuck the key in the ignition. When the outboard sprang to life, it sounded like a lawnmower.

"You can do this, right, Victor?" Ryan asked. "You know how to get there in the dark?"

"Relax, I was in the Navy for four years."

"That's good, because I don't know shit about marine navigation."

Victor unfolded a chart of Santa Catalina Island and the San Pedro Channel, and pulled up the GPS app on his cellphone. "You wanna untie us?"

The two DEA agents left the marina and headed toward the Outer Harbor. Their small craft passed Terminal Island, and a gust of wind brought the smell of diesel exhaust from the massive shipping container complex that worked around the clock. Ryan watched the frenetic activity illuminated by a galaxy of Night-Sun spotlights. Semi-trailer trucks were everywhere, jockeying for position, and forklifts scurried around like giant cockroaches. Big cranes, hundreds of feet high, leaned out over the ships like Praying Mantises, lifting containers off the decks and lowering them onto empty flatbeds. The sound of engines, warning klaxons, and men shouting echoed across the water. Beyond the terminal, they passed a container ship lying at anchor, riding low in the channel and waiting to be unloaded. The vessel, the length of three football fields, with a mountain of containers stacked on its deck, towered above them. Ryan gazed up at the name illuminated on the stern—*Jinhui*—unsure what country it had come from.

When they cleared the harbor, the light and noise faded, complete darkness descended, and the sharp smell of saltwater replaced the diesel odor. The rough, open water made Ryan nauseous and he tried to steady himself on the pitching, rolling boat. By the time they approached Catalina two hours later, he was ready to vomit.

"Look at that," Victor said when they saw the light streaming out of the *Exchange Rate's* portholes. "I wonder what that sucker cost." He cut the engine and their boat drifted for a moment until he threw out the anchor.

The two agents used their night-vision glasses to get a close look at the majestic yacht.

"It doesn't look to me like they're getting ready to unload a drug shipment," Victor remarked when the huge boat finally went dark an hour later. "They're going to sleep."

"Don't worry," Ryan reassured him. "Something's definitely gonna happen—they're probably waiting until morning."

Ryan and Victor spent the rest of the night sipping coffee from a thermos and watching the yacht in two-hour shifts. By sunrise, both men were stiff, cold, and tired. Victor raised the awning over the cockpit and stowed their gear—Kevlar vests, the AR15 equipped with an optical sight, and their radios and camera—inside the cuddy cabin. Then he baited the hooks on the two fishing poles lying on the deck of the boat and played out the lines. "Do I look like I came out here to fish, or do I look like a tired undercover agent?" he asked Ryan while he placed the poles in the rod holders at the stern. "Stay back under the awning so no one can see you with the glasses."

An hour later, the big yacht came to life, and at 7:30 a.m. it raised anchor and started in toward Paradise Cove. Ryan hid under the awning and watched through his binoculars as the boat stopped 1,000 yards off the sand and the crew prepared to launch a Zodiac from the swim platform.

"I dunno," Victor said, fiddling with a fishing rod and trying not to be obvious about looking at the yacht. "What are they doing with that damn rubber dinghy? They can't transport a load of drugs in that, it's too small. This doesn't look like right."

"They've loaded something on," Ryan said, and refocused his glasses. "It looks like some kind of wire cage." He leaned against the door to the cuddy cabin to steady himself and struggled to track the Zodiac as it skimmed over the water. He studied the two people in the Zodiac and began to have his own doubts. Where he expected to see a band of tough-looking Mexican cartel soldiers brandishing automatic weapons, he saw a clean-shaven man in a white steward's uniform steering, and a young kid riding in the bow. Ryan was baffled. "A white uniform?" he muttered. "What the hell?" He stared so intently through the glasses that eyestrain made little flashes of light float across his line of vision. He had never seen a Mexican drug smuggler dressed in pressed white pants and a white shirt with decorative epaulets. Ryan watched them tie up at the small dock and unload the cage.

"Are you getting this?" Victor said. "We're screwed. Whatever this is about, it's not a drug drop."

Ryan couldn't believe it. Had Operation Bird's Eye gotten it wrong? This definitely wasn't the outcome he had expected when he and Victor were assigned to BEST, the Border Enforcement Security Taskforce.

The two DEA agents had passed through the security gate at March Field in Riverside, California, late one weekday morning a month earlier. On the inside, the vast Air Force base looked abandoned. Following directions, they drove along empty streets, past deserted barracks and administration buildings with broken windows and entrances covered with plywood. The huge aircraft hangars were silent, their massive rolling doors sealed shut. On the runway, several steel-gray air tankers had been mothballed. Parked in a tight formation, their jet engine intakes were capped with red covers.

"This is creepy," Ryan said.

"It looks like the whole base is decommissioned," Victor replied.

Ryan drove on until they came to a group of nondescript, one-story tan buildings with a perimeter of barbwire fence. Several cars were parked on the blacktop next to a sign that announced *Customs and Border Patrol – Air and Marine Operations Center.*

Armed guards stopped them at the entrance. After the two DEA agents showed their IDs and gave up their pistols, they were ushered into a conference room with cold air blasting from the air conditioning system. Ryan saw a group of XL-sized men with military-style haircuts, fire-hydrant necks, and bulging biceps sitting around an oblong conference table. On their shoulders, they wore arm patches from the Coast Guard and several law enforcement agencies including LAPD, Los Angeles County Sheriff's Department, Los Angeles Port Police, and Long Beach Police Department. Ryan also recognized men he knew from other three-letter Federal law enforcement agencies.

The man standing at the front of the room wore a half-zipped jacket. He glanced at Ryan and Victor when they entered, checked his clipboard, and said, "Okay, let's get started. Sorry it's so cold in here, but we're cooling a lot of computers and communications equipment, and in these old buildings we don't have the luxury of zone air conditioning. Help yourselves to coffee, it may warm you up." He looked at the men sitting around the table and continued, "Welcome to the first meeting of BEST. My name is Ted Parker. I'm a detection enforcement officer with Customs and Border Patrol and I'll be your task force leader for what we've named Operation Bird's Eye. It's no secret that we have a big problem with drugs coming into Southern California by water. The number of shipments dropped on our shores by the cartels is increasing, and every month they're moving farther up the coast. What used to be a problem just in San Diego County has now spread as far north as Catalina and the Channel Islands. They're also scaling up, using boats with deep-V offshore racing hulls and outboard engines with a thousand horsepower to move their goods. Some of them are coming direct from Mexico and some are local boats picking up cargo from larger craft parked offshore in U.S. waters. We've even seen a couple of crude submarines, although I can't imagine how anyone could survive for more than five minutes in one of those tin cans."

Two officers from the Highway Patrol entered the room, and one apologized, "Sorry we're late."

Parker nodded at them and continued. "The Coast Guard has primary responsibility for drug interdiction and they have their hands full."

"Things are definitely escalating," one of the Coast Guard men interjected, "Two weeks ago, we tried to stop smugglers in a fast boat off the coast of Santa Barbara. They rammed one of our tactical pursuit vessels and a chief petty officer was knocked into the water. They ran over him and he died."

Ryan had had his own experience with smugglers coming in off the water. A few weeks earlier, State Park Rangers had called the DEA in the middle of the day to request assistance in searching for the occupants of a disabled panga that had washed ashore on a Malibu beach. By the time he arrived, officers from the Sheriff's Department and the Highway Patrol had already captured a Mexican national and snagged several large bundles of marijuana floating in the water. The boat was impounded, but the rest of its crew was never found. From the DEA's point of view, it was a low-level incident, but it did get some press coverage. The following day, Ryan's group supervisor warned him, "Do not, I repeat, *do not,* get your picture in the *Los Angeles Times* wearing a DEA vest."

"So," Parker went on, "today marks the start of a joint SoCal law-enforcement effort to stop the flow of drugs. Customs and Border Patrol has been using Guardian drones for a couple of years to monitor maritime activity around both coasts, and for Operation Bird's Eye we're going to dedicate one to just look at everything coming up by water from Mexico."

"What's a Guardian?" a Long Beach police officer asked. "Is that like a Predator?"

"Yeah, it's the civilian equivalent," Parker said. "It has all the optics, but doesn't carry missiles or other weapons. If the Guardian spots something that looks like it's enroute to California, we'll notify the members of the task force. The Coast Guard and the DEA will have the lead on any incident, and they'll call for backup as needed from other agencies." Parker pointed at Ryan and Victor. "These men are our DEA liaison. Can you guys talk a little bit about your protocol, and what you're trying to accomplish?"

Ryan stood up. "Ryan Daniels, Special Agent, DEA." He gestured to Victor. "This is my partner Victor. Here's the problem. We often end up working at cross-purposes with the Coast Guard, because we'd prefer not to prevent the bad guys from bringing drugs onshore." Ryan glanced at the three men from the Coast Guard, sitting across the table. "We know your job is to stop them in the water, before they touch the U.S. mainland, but that doesn't work for us. When you search a suspicious vessel and arrest everyone, we have no chance to find out who's waiting at the drop point, or where the shipment's going. I guarantee that you'll never seize enough drugs to make a difference, and all you're doing is grabbing low-level delivery boys. We have to find out where the cargo goes when it comes ashore."

"We need to work our way up the food chain," Victor added. "If they're dropping something on a beach, someone has to be waiting to pick it up, with trucks or other vehicles big enough to carry a ton of marijuana bales and whatever other drugs they've sent. If they leave it on Catalina or on one of the Channel Islands, then there'll be other boats coming to get it. After the pickup, they have to get the cargo out of sight as soon as possible, so the first stop will be a stash house. Later, they'll move everything to a distribution center, repackage it, and send it out all over the country."

"Each destination we can identify," Ryan continued, "is a step up the ladder to the big bosses and kingpins. If we can track the drugs all the way through the distribution channels, we may be able to tap into the entire network and grab some top-level people. That's why a premature seizure of the drugs on the water is the last thing we want to happen."

"You're going to *follow* the drugs?" one of the Coast Guard men asked.

"We'll give it our best shot," Victor said. "The trick is to be there when the cargo is dropped."

"Actually," Ryan said, "we have to be there *before* the drugs are dropped."

"That's why this has to be a joint effort," Victor said. "It's going to take some lucky timing and good surveillance, and we'll need backup from local agencies. If we suspect drugs are about to be unloaded somewhere, the first thing we'll call for is helicopter surveillance."

"And that means you'll have to be in the air fast," Ryan said.

"It's going to depend on how much notice we get, and where the drop occurs." A Port Police officer said. "Our AeroBureau has a crew ready 24/7, and we can get to areas near Long Beach and Catalina within a few minutes. If you're talking about the Channel Islands, that's a totally different story. It's not even our jurisdiction."

"Our first call will go to whatever agency has jurisdiction where the drop is made," Ryan said. "When the drugs hit the road, we'll need help with ground surveillance, and that would most likely be from the County Sheriffs or the Highway Patrol."

"If the drone spots something of interest," Parker said, "we'll notify the Coast Guard and DEA ASAP. The Coast Guard will assist in tracking the vessel, and if we can give you enough notice before a drop, it'll be the DEA's responsibility to organize surveillance and call for whatever backup it needs."

"And if it all goes to shit," a Coast Guard man said, "we'll be there to stop them in the water, like we always do."

"*Booyah!*" someone in the group said, and Parker threw him a look.

"Right," Ryan grinned. "If it goes to shit, you can still send your little boats after them."

"Okay, that's it for today," Parker said. "We'll be headquartered at the Coast Guard station in San Pedro, but for this first meeting we thought you should come out here and get a look at the part of Customs and Border Patrol that no one ever sees. No one here wears a green uniform, and our job isn't to chase immigrants through the brush. What we do is vertical border protection, using state of the art surveillance to track and identify every noncommercial aircraft in or near U.S. airspace. That means we monitor about 25,000 aircraft a day, and if we don't like the looks of one of them, we can stop it." Parker stood up. "Follow me—we'll take a quick tour."

He led the men out of the conference room and down a hallway that dead-ended at a steel security door with armed officers. Parker placed the palm of his hand on a scanner, waited until the door swung open, and led the group into a darkened room, one wall of which was glass from floor to ceiling.

Through the glass, Ryan saw something that reminded him of

Mission Control in Houston—a cavernous room with dozens of men sitting at computer terminals. They faced a wall covered with a huge electronic map showing the United States with a geographical perimeter several hundred miles in all directions beyond the border.

"This is what we call the surveillance floor," Parker said. "On that screen, we're tracking 24/7, in real time, every general aviation aircraft flying over the U.S., and any aircraft within 100 miles of our border. As you can imagine, our southern border gets most of the attention. We've got sophisticated software and a database to help us identify each plane, tell us where it's headed, and in most cases, where it's been during the last thirty days. If we have to, we can interface with the U.S. air defense system and with most law enforcement agencies across the country."

Ryan gazed at the thousands of white and colored dots on the map, some moving, some stationary. It looked like a cloud of gnats coming off a lake on a summer evening in Indiana. "Each dot's an aircraft?"

"That's right," Parker said, "We're processing info from hundreds of radar units and other sensors strung out around a perimeter that runs across central Mexico, west to the Hawaiian Islands, back across Canada, and out around the Bahamas. Each one of the men you see on the surveillance floor is monitoring a particular sector. The software notifies him if there is an unidentified aircraft in his area. Anything we see coming north across the 24th parallel from Central America is considered possible drug traffic."

"How about the drone operations," someone asked. "Where does that happen?"

"The drone pilots work down the hall," Parker said. "We've got several Guardians covering specific areas on the East Coast, the Caribbean corridor and the West Coast, and as I said, we plan to dedicate one to Operation Bird's Eye. Drone ops aren't as impressive as this," he said, pointing to the electronic map of the United States. "It's a lot less automated. It's just pilots sitting at their flight consoles monitoring images sent back by the cameras on the drones."

"So how good is your water surveillance capability?" a Sheriff's deputy asked.

"Boats are a lot more problematic than aircraft." Parker said. "It's a huge ocean and sometimes we just don't see them. If we do, we rarely have background and registry info, especially on all the small boats that pop out of the west coast of Mexico. If we can't identify a suspicious boat, we notify Mexican authorities, for whatever that's worth. If it's a craft headed toward U.S. waters the Coast Guard is alerted, but even they can't interdict every boat coming north, so most of them are never intercepted. That's why we've set up this task force. We'll see if it improves our catch rate."

The group asked a few more questions and watched the little white dots move around the electronic map until Parker escorted them out of the room. In the hallway, a large woman in a blue flight suit came toward them. Her name, DeAndra White, was displayed on a small badge above her left breast.

"This is Surveillance Officer White," Parker said. "She joined us recently from the Air Force and will be piloting one shift of the Bird's Eye surveillance."

The woman nodded, flashed the group a quick, tense smile, but said nothing. She continued past the group with her eyes focused on the floor.

Once back in the conference room, Parker told the group, "I'll distribute a contact list and we'll schedule a practice day next week in San Pedro to run through some tabletop surveillance and interdiction scenarios. Finally, let me just remind you that the state and local agencies participating in the task force get a share of the proceeds from any cars, boats, or other property confiscated by the Marshals in a drug bust. Keep that in mind. A big seizure can do wonders for your budget, especially these days."

Several days after the BEST meeting in Riverside, the surveillance drone spotted a large yacht moving north from Culiacán in Mexico. The boat's ownership was investigated and traced to a possible Sinaloan Cartel boss. Once it was determined that it was heading for U.S. waters, Ryan and the others were called to an urgent briefing at the Coast Guard station in the San Pedro Harbor. It appeared that the task force might have sighted its first drug shipment headed for the U.S.

"These are pictures of the boat transmitted today from the drone," Parker announced. He passed the photos around the table to the men from the various agencies.

"This is supposed to be a drug boat?" a Port Police officer asked, gazing at the photo of the sleek craft throwing up a huge wake off San Diego. "It looks like a private yacht."

"We've tracked it for two days," Parker said. "It came out of Culiacán and it's registered to someone with Swiss and Mexican citizenship who may have ties to the Sinaloa Cartel. Is that good enough? If they're carrying a drug cargo, as we suspect, we should find out in the next twenty-four hours. A Coast Guard Cutter is just over their horizon, tracking them. Right now, they're south of San Diego. They may be planning to make a drop somewhere up the coast, at sea, or maybe on Catalina." He flashed his laser pointer at a map on the wall and made a red circle around the island, twenty-five miles southwest of Los Angeles. "If we're lucky, we'll get enough advance notice so the DEA surveillance team can move into position before they can unload." He glanced at Ryan and Victor. "You guys ready to go on short notice?"

"We're ready," Victor responded.

"I don't buy it," the Port Police officer said. "This boat has to be worth millions. No matter how rich these guys are, they won't risk having a boat like that confiscated. They don't send a luxury yacht to deliver drugs—they send some piece of junk that isn't worth anything."

"Maybe they're trying to fake us out," Parker said.

"It sure would be great to grab a prize like that," someone said.

When they walked out of the meeting, Ryan slapped Victor on the back. "This could be big," he said. "Really big. There's a huge shipment of drugs headed our way and we'll be there when they unload it."

"But the guy from the Port Police had a point," Victor said. "Doesn't it bother you that it's a mega-yacht?"

"Hell no. Parker's right. It's a perfect cover. It's brilliant. Who would question a boat like that? And if one of those crappy little fast boats can move 2,000 pounds of marijuana, how many tons of bad stuff can a huge yacht like that carry?"

"I'd feel better if it was something different, maybe some old freighter."

"No way. An old freighter would be about as obvious as that battleship." Ryan pointed across the channel to the 900-foot long gray hulk of the *USS Iowa*, now a floating museum. A tour bus with a group of veterans had just arrived and a group of old-timers leaned on their canes as they descended the stairs and walked on weak legs into the parking lot to gaze at the once-mighty battleship. "Mark my words, Victor," Ryan repeated, "this is gonna be huge."

Now, as Ryan stood rocking on the small fishing boat off Catalina Island, watching the Zodiac with the man in the white uniform pull away from the dock, his doubts were growing. "He's leaving the kid on the dock," he said to Victor, "along with the cage, or whatever it is."

"It looks like an animal cage," Victor said, "but who cares. This is a false alarm, we've wasted our time." He started the old Evinrude and swung the boat around toward San Pedro. "Let's get off this miserable little tub. Call the Port Police and tell them to stand down."

"Wait a minute, Victor, hold on," Ryan pleaded. "The boy's still on the dock. Let's just wait and see what happens." It was a critical moment, and Ryan was reluctant to give up on the operation. Since the task force first spotted the big yacht, he had been praying it might be the beginning of the case that would lead him to a promotion and a bump in pay— something he desperately needed.

Ryan remembered his first day on the job at the DEA. How long ago was it? Three years? It seemed like an eternity. A newly-minted federal agent, he had sat in his tiny cubicle on the twentieth floor of the Roybal Federal Building, home of the Los Angeles Field Division and wondered if he had made a mistake. The Metropolitan Detention Center, a white granite monolith next door, loomed up in front of his window, blocking the view. The prisoners were out in the exercise cage on the 15th floor, and he listened to their shouts while he considered his future at the DEA.

"If you wanna participate in law enforcement at the highest level, come work for us," a DEA agent had told him in a recruiting interview. "It's global. We're fighting the drug war all over the world."

At the time, it seemed like just the ticket to escape a humdrum life in Terre Haute, a sleepy city of 70,000 on the eastern bank of the Wabash River.

The agent had looked him over and said, "You're too clean cut to work undercover. You have to grow up on the streets to do that, but you could work general enforcement. If you need more excitement, you can move into special ops. We have agents in sixty countries, and if you really wanna get down and dirty, we have guys wearing camo and slogging through the rain forests in Central America. Put in three years in the states and then you can go abroad."

Ryan could barely contain his excitement. At the time, the GS-7 starter salary of $63,000 had sounded like a fortune.

"Are you interested?" the agent had asked.

"Hell yes," Ryan told him. The job was a godsend to a run-of-the-mill quarterback who had just graduated Indiana State University with unexceptional grades, a BS in Criminal Justice, and no idea what he wanted to do.

After Ryan signed on, the DEA sent him to their training academy at the Marine Corps Base at Quantico. The first weeks were a lot like college, except everything was about law enforcement. Ryan went through physical fitness and defensive tactics training, and learned about evasive driving. He had never even owned a pistol, but became qualified to use handguns, shotguns, assault rifles, and even a machine gun. What he liked the most was the instruction on covert surveillance and undercover operations. What he liked least was learning how to prepare the detailed paperwork necessary to obtain state and federal wiretaps. Ryan shared a dormitory room with a former police officer from Las Cruces, New Mexico, and listened late into the night to his accounts of human-trafficking incidents on the Mexican border.

Ryan was still living the dream when he graduated the Academy, received his badge, and chose a Glock 43 as his personal weapon. Reality set in a week later when he was assigned to the Los Angeles field office and discovered that the cost of living in the City of Angels was almost double that of Terre Haute. So much for the $63,000 salary. He shared a tiny apartment in Glendale with another rookie agent, used his savings to buy a used car for the one-hour drive to the Roybal Building, and lived on cheap junk food. As soon as he started work, Ryan asked how to accelerate his move up the salary ranks.

"You put in the time and work your way up," his group supervisor told him. "In a couple of years, maybe three, you'll be a GS-9. With adjustments for living in Los Angeles, that'll get you about $70,000. At some point, you'll have a chance to make an important case. If it's big enough, and you don't screw it up, you can submit a merit promotion package. Merit promotions can take you all the way up to a GS-13, and that's pretty high. GS-14 and 15 is for the top brass."

Just as the agent had predicted, after three years, Ryan had progressed to a GS-9 and was making $71,600 a year. With that money, he could have lived like a king in Terre Haute, but in Southern California, it was still nothing. He felt he was almost at the poverty level in a city where everyone drove an expensive car and ate $100 sushi dinners. His desire for a raise had become even more urgent after he met Sharon, a paralegal at a law firm in Orange County. He liked her a lot, and hoped to start seeing her on a regular basis. She was attracted to him, a young law enforcement agent with a badge and a gun, but he had to spend money to keep her interested. Sharon liked going out to dinner and loved dancing in the late-night clubs. She dropped hints about little gifts, things he could give her, and had mentioned how wonderful it would be if they could go away together for the weekend. She talked about Cabo San Lucas; a spot she'd heard was very romantic. Ryan kept making excuses—he didn't have the money to spend. He was still picking her up in his beat-up old car.

When the BEST assignment came up, Ryan saw divine intervention. This was a golden opportunity to intercept a major drug shipment, make a big case, and justify a merit promotion. When the big yacht was spotted coming out of Mexico, Ryan was certain this was his chance. He imagined surveilling the transfer of a huge cache of drugs and tracking it first to a stash house and then on to a major distribution center. He would be the first man through the door, leading a team of agents, making important arrests, seizing truckloads of marijuana and cocaine, and confiscating millions of dollars in cash. And that would be just the beginning. On a roll, he would seize cell phones, trace numbers, and set up wiretaps. He would identify other narco-criminals, lead more DEA men on takedowns, and make more arrests. When he filled out his Six—the DEA's internal report on an ongoing investigation—it would run two dozen pages. His work would unravel a monumental drug distribution network covering the entire West Coast, maybe even the whole United States. It would be a big case—no, a *huge* case, and the DEA would recognize him for his outstanding effort in bringing down a vast web of drug smugglers. The merit promotion would be a slam-dunk, and he would leapfrog two levels on the Civil Service pay scale at once. Ryan Daniels would become a legend in the DEA, his picture hung on the Wall of Heroes in the division conference room. And once his promotion came through, Ryan would buy a BMW—not the cheap 3 Series, but a silver 650i with the big engine. Even before he got his raise, he planned to take out a loan and whisk Sharon off to Cabo. They would go for a week, not just a weekend, stay in a suite and have breakfast on the beach. That was how he had imagined it.

Now, bobbing around on the little surveillance boat in the cool early morning, Ryan was confronting a much different reality. Victor had been right. The big yacht hadn't unloaded a cargo of drugs. All he had in his sights was a kid sitting on a dock with some kind of an animal cage. Ryan scanned the water once more, trying to identify someone, anyone, waiting to make a rendezvous, but he didn't see anything unusual. A couple of boats trolled back and forth, dragging their lines through the water, a few others were bottom fishing around the rocks, and one beat-up craft had just weighed anchor and headed toward the mainland.

"Maybe we should go in and arrest the boy," Ryan said. "We could question him about the boat."

"Are you crazy?" Victor said. "We're going to waste our time arresting a kid? How old is he? Ten? Twelve?"

"He probably works for the cartel. Maybe he's older than he looks."

"What are you going to do with him? Huh? He's a minor. You plan on taking him into custody? That means a trip to the Detention Center and hours of paperwork. For what? There's nothing to find out. He's too young to be a cartel soldier. We've been on this damn boat for fourteen hours and I say it's time to go home."

"I dunno…"

"I'll tell you what," Victor said. "Notify the Sheriff's Department on Catalina. Let them pick him up. We can always go back to talk to him later."

"Alright," Ryan said. "I give up. But before we leave, let me check in with the drone pilot and make sure we're not missing something."

Before she even began her 6:00 a.m. shift at the drone flight console in the Air and Marine Operations Center, DeAndra White was having a bad day. She had barely slept the night before and was exhausted and depressed. The nightmares were getting worse. In her dreams, a boy, about the size of her son, appeared each night to torment her. She struggled to see him clearly, but could never bring him into focus. In the turmoil of his visitations, she was certain he was trying to rebuke her for what she had done. After each nightmare, she awoke in a panic, her sheets soaked with sweat. Unable to go back to sleep, DeAndra would lie in bed until dawn, staring at the ceiling and trembling.

"Morning, Davis," she said to the surveillance officer who worked the graveyard shift. She glanced at the monitor and saw the big yacht from Mexico anchored in the water, riding the early morning swells off Catalina Island.

"Handing off," Davis said before he stood and stretched.

DeAndra settled into the leather pilot's chair, still warm from Davis' body. "Anything?" she asked.

"No. They dropped anchor yesterday late afternoon and I watched them all night. They haven't moved."

She took control of the drone, stared at the screen, and waited. An hour and a half later, she saw activity on the yacht. DeAndra watched it move closer to the beach and launch a rubber Zodiac with two men, one wearing a white uniform. The black boat travelled the short distance to a dock where they unloaded something and one of the men climbed up onto the dock. The man remaining in the Zodiac, the one wearing the uniform, turned it around and headed back to the yacht.

DeAndra increased the magnification of the drone's camera. The Guardian's on-board color TV was powerful enough to give her a good close up and she saw that the person on the dock was a boy, not a man. She leaned forward in her chair, her face inches from the monitor, and felt the blood run cold in her veins. She was looking at the presence who had been haunting her dreams.

She was still riveted to the screen when the call from the DEA agent was transferred to her from the operations manager on the surveillance floor. "This is Agent Daniels with the Bird's Eye task force," he said. "I'm out on the water near Paradise Cove."

"Surveillance Officer White here."

"Officer White?" Ryan said. "Didn't we see you in the hall last month when we were getting a tour of the facility? How're you doing?"

"Okay," DeAndra said. "What can I do for you?"

"You're tracking the yacht?"

"Since I came on duty at six."

"Do you see any unusual activity? Could there be something going on that we can't see? Is anyone approaching the beach from the land side? We're expecting a drug drop, but all we've got is a kid sitting with something—maybe an animal cage—that they left on the dock. From water level we don't—"

"There is a boy," DeAndra interrupted in a brusque tone. "And he is by himself. You got that right, but it's not a drug drop."

"Are you sure? How do you know?"

"Am I sure?" Her voice began to rise. "Do you see kilos of coke stacked on the dock? Nooo. Bales of marijuana floating in the water? Nooo. Any contraband, anywhere? No again. Just a boy on a dock. Right? It doesn't look like a drug drop because it's not. Plain and simple." DeAndra paused to take a deep breath and struggled to calm down. "That's it." She was almost shouting now. "There's nothing suspicious to report. Period." While she spoke, she stared at the image of the boy on the monitor. He was pacing around the dock.

"Hello?" the DEA agent said. "You still there?"

"Yes." She wondered why he was bothering her.

"So that's it?"

"That's what I said, that's it!" she screamed into the phone. "I can't create a drug drop where there is none." She retracted the camera lens to scan the nearby water and saw that the yacht was now underway, throwing up a huge white wake. "The boat's leaving," she said. "It's headed south, maybe back to Mexico. There's nothing more I can tell you." As she spoke, DeAndra saw an official text message coming across her communications screen and paused to read it. "Look, we're done here," she said. "My intel supervisor has just advised me that your surveillance is being temporarily suspended. We've got an emergency situation developing in Arizona. A border patrol officer has just been killed and I have to send the drone over there. Nice to talk to you, uh, Agent uh—" DeAndra disconnected although she was sure the DEA agent had more to say.

The spot in Arizona, across the border from Nogales, Mexico, was 385 miles away and it would take about two hours to reposition the Guardian, but DeAndra wasn't ready to move it. What she wanted to do was continue to scrutinize the boy. Adjusting the zoom lens until his face filled her monitor screen, she watched him turn his head and look up at the sky. DeAndra shuddered. He knew she was watching him and he was gazing back at her! She saw his lips moving, he was talking to her, but just as in her dreams, she couldn't make out what he was saying. She pressed the palms of her hands against her eyes.

Was that a kid? Did we just kill a kid?

Yeah, I think that was a kid, a boy.

DeAndra was coming unglued and felt helpless to do anything about it.

"*Chinga!*" Felix cursed. The *Truckin* had already travelled almost half way back to Long Beach from Catalina, and all he could think about was the prized Motagua Valley beaded lizard that he had left behind. How much effort had been expended to capture and deliver it to Culiacán? It had come all the way from a remote spot in Guatemala. He had seen the cage right there, sitting on the dock, waiting for him to pick it up. How many nights had he dreamed about having that lizard? How much time and money had he spent building it a perfect habitat? The reptile had been almost within arm's reach and now he had abandoned it, heading home without it.

Felix began to second-guess himself. Had he overreacted? Why would there be surveillance on Paradise Cove? It was a spot for swimming and diving, and nothing more. Was some law enforcement agency watching the *Exchange Rate*? How would they have even known it was there? Besides, it wasn't carrying contraband. It was a luxury yacht. And the craft he had spotted was too small—who would use such a tiny boat for surveillance? It was ridiculous. There was barely room on it to move around. Perhaps he had jumped to the wrong conclusion. He ran through a dozen reasons to justify going back, but it all came down to the fact that he couldn't just abandon his lizard. He could not go home without it. His intuition, his sixth sense had always kept him out of trouble in the past, but now he was overriding it. He had to return for his prize.

Felix turned the *Truckin* back toward Catalina and gunned the engine. It would take almost an hour to return to Paradise Cove—would the lizard still be there? All he had to do was come up alongside the dock, stop for a few seconds, and grab the cage. He cursed his lazy son for not coming with him. An extra set of hands would have helped, but Felix could do it himself. He was self-reliant, he always had been. When he got home, he would have a serious talk with Daniel. No, he would have more than a talk with him—he would teach him a lesson. How had he allowed his son to become so lazy and spoiled?

On the way back to Catalina, Felix reminded himself to be careful. He decided to drop anchor and study the situation through his glasses before he went anywhere near the dock. If anything seemed out of place, if the same boat was still there watching the beach, then he wouldn't take any risks and would head home. He glanced at his watch. Later in the morning, he had a dump truck coming over the border crossing at San Ysidro. The hydraulic piston and rod used to raise the bed of the truck had been removed and 62 kilos of the highest-grade cocaine were stashed inside the barrel. After it was "stepped on," or cut—using bulking agents like baby laxatives—the coke would be worth over $2 million on the street. Felix had never tried this trick before, but the mobile X-ray scanning equipment used by the border patrol for vehicle inspections would have difficulty penetrating the thick metal hydraulic cylinder. In an hour, it would be time to call the driver for an update. Felix said a silent prayer to *Santa Muerte*—the patron saint of smugglers—for the safe passage of the cocaine. When he touched the cellphone in his pocket, he realized his mistake. He had meant to take a burner when he left his house, something he could toss away at the end of the day.

Somehow, in the midst of his anger over his son's failure to come along, he had grabbed his personal phone. Felix shook his head. He was getting careless. Carrying his new Apple iPhone loaded with all the confidential contact numbers of his key operatives was stupid. Really stupid.

"No!" Victor exclaimed when the old outboard sputtered and died. He tried the ignition button twice, but the engine turned over without starting. "I don't believe it."

"What?" Ryan said.

Victor bent down and unscrewed the cap on the gas tank. "We're empty."

"Empty? Out of gas?" Ryan screamed, "*Fuuck.* They rent this crappy little boat for us and we don't even get a full tank of gas? What are we supposed to do? Swim back? We're ten miles from shore."

"We'll have to call the Coast Guard," Victor said.

At that moment, drifting on a disabled boat in the strong current of the San Pedro Channel, Ryan was certain he wouldn't be taking his girlfriend Sharon to Cabo any time soon.

DeAndra thought the boy on the dock wasn't remarkable, he was just another skinny kid like all the undernourished children she had watched from the skies over Afghanistan, but she was mesmerized, she couldn't take her eyes off of him. How old was he? The same age as her son? The same age as the child she had killed? *Was* it the child she had killed? Yes, it *was!* What was he doing on a dock on Catalina Island in the United States? DeAndra's thoughts were in a tailspin. She rubbed her eyes and tried to think clearly.

It had been two years since her tour of duty as a captain in the Air Force was cut short. What began as a promising military career had ended with a determination that she was psychologically and emotionally unfit for further service. They gave her an honorable discharge and sent her to see a therapist twice a week at the VA hospital in North Las Vegas.

At the time, operating becoming an RPA operator—a remotely piloted aircraft—had seemed like the perfect move in her career. Some said that piloting a drone was a dead end in the military and called it the "Chair Force," but DeAndra didn't care. Someone mentioned the long hours of boredom punctuated by minutes of high stress, but all that mattered to her was that the pay was good and that she wouldn't have to face another foreign deployment. Becoming a drone pilot meant she could stay in the Air Force as a single mother and raise her troubled son in the suburban confines of Creech Air Force Base outside Las Vegas. She didn't even need real flight experience. In fact, they told her the gamers, the kids who grew up playing video competitions, made the best drone pilots. After several months, DeAndra had qualified to pilot a $15 million Reaper armed with Hellfire air-to-ground missiles and the larger, laser guided bombs.

Each morning, she put on an Air Force flight suit, sent her son off to school, and drove ten minutes to the cluster of faded air-conditioned orange trailers that housed the drone flight consoles at the far end of the base. Once inside the trailer, through the miracle of a satellite communications link, DeAndra was transported 7,500 miles away to the skies over Afghanistan. It didn't matter what time it was, the drone's optics and infrared capability saw everything, day or night, dusk or dawn. For the next ten hours, the distractions of her daily life and the concerns about her son faded away while she piloted the Reaper and her sensor operator controlled the cameras, radar, and targeting systems. Sitting side by side in a semi-dark virtual cockpit, in front of a communications console with an array of computer screens, they drank energy drinks to stay alert. DeAndra, never a small woman, had begun to gain weight.

Ninety-five percent of their time was devoted to "overwatch"—

surveillance and reconnaissance—while they searched for Taliban combatants moving across the sand and scrubby hills. They were supervised by mission intelligence officers located in a command center somewhere else in the world—men they spoke to but never saw. When a call came in from an attack controller on the battleground in Afghanistan, instructing them to drop bombs or fire missiles at a target, the adrenaline kicked in. Sometimes the orders were specific—"Drop a guided bomb on this exact spot." Sometimes DeAndra and her sensor operator had wide latitude—"Just kill those guys."

Before the authorization to fire came, they often loitered in the sky, watching their prey, for hours or even days at a time, waiting for their targets to separate from the other men, women, and children around them, trying to ensure that innocents were not around when a strike occurred. Eventually, the personalized nature of the killing began to bother DeAndra. Even though she was sitting thousands of miles away, she had begun to feel an eerie bond with the people she was targeting, and watching them live and then die was beginning to trouble her. The "squirters," the ones who ran away from the incoming missiles, were the worst.

"You have to anticipate the sonic boom time," her instructor had warned her. "Depending on the angle of your shot, it can be several seconds between the boom and the impact. When that happens, your target will run. Everyone in Afghanistan knows that when they hear a boom, they should run because we're overhead. There aren't any fat Afghans, and some of them can really run fast."

More than once, DeAndra had sat transfixed, watching a victim react to the sonic boom and look up toward the sky, seconds before the "splash," or impact of the missile. Afterward, when the smoke cleared, the image of the human being had disappeared and all she saw was a crater in the ground. After routinely raining missiles and laser-guided bombs down from the sky, DeAndra found it increasingly difficult to return to daily life at the end of her shift. She wanted to share her emotions with others and talk about how she was feeling, but discovered that no one was willing to discuss drone operations. An officer told DeAndra to "shut up and cope."

On her last day of active duty, she and the sensor operator had been tasked with striking a high-level Taliban fighter standing in a compound near a building. In the final countdown, the sensor had confirmed their aim point and kept the laser spot on the target. DeAndra had called out, "Three, two, one, rifle," and then pressed the red button on the joystick and fired the missile. In the seconds before impact, she looked in disbelief at something that came around the corner of the building. It was small and two-legged, and she was certain it was the image of a human being. She watched as it disappeared in the splash of the missile.

"Was that a kid?" DeAndra asked her sensor. "Did we just kill a kid?"

"Was it?" he replied. "I don't know."

"Yes. I think it was a child. A boy. We killed a little boy," DeAndra said.

"It wasn't a fucking kid," the Intel Coordinator interrupted, watching the silent detonation of the missile on a video feed thousands of miles away.

"Well then, what was it? DeAndra asked.

"Maybe an animal," the Intel Coordinator replied. "No way to tell from here."

The image had appeared quickly, indistinct because it was dark and they were using infrared, but there was no doubt in DeAndra's mind—it was a small person, about the same size as her twelve-year-old son. She was numb. She had killed an innocent child.

When she left the Air Force, DeAndra found a less demanding job with Customs and Border Protection, where they chose to overlook her psychological issues because they needed experienced drone pilots.

She moved from one Air Force base in Nevada to another in Southern California, where her new job was flying a Guardian drone. Two years passed, and neither cognitive processing therapy at the VA Hospital nor any of several different anti-depressants had helped DeAndra. At night, her dreams were troubled. During the day, she lost concentration, suffered through dark moods, and often cried.

She felt better about piloting a Customs and Border Protection drone without bombs and missiles, thankful not to have to lase a human target and watch the splash of a deadly explosion. At first, when she scanned the waters off the west coast of Mexico and Southern California for the movement of illegals and drugs, she felt almost like a normal person. The problem was, as time passed, her nightmares became more frequent and the image of the boy began haunt her. Soon the Mexicans, Guatemalans, and Hondurans on her screen became indistinguishable from the Pashtuns, Tajiks, and Hazaras she had tracked in Afghanistan, and her life deteriorated to the point where she was just struggling to hang on.

DeAndra sat motionless in front of her flight console, clenched the joystick, and continued to stare at her monitor. The boy sitting on the dock looked so familiar. The dark blue water off Catalina Island became the evening sand on the dreary Kandahar tableland. Now the boy was outside a square building built of mud-bricks, surrounded by the broken walls of a compound. A few sheep and goats milled around him. When he heard the sonic boom of the incoming missile, the boy stood up and began to run. DeAndra trembled. Perspiration ran off her body and soaked her clothes. She stood up. "I have to take an emergency pee break," she announced, and fled from the room. In the bathroom, she locked the door and turned on the faucets so that no one could hear her panicked sobs.

Felix cut his engine and let the *Truckin* drift toward the cove, moving with the current and the breeze that had come up, scanning the area around the beach with his binoculars. The fishing boats were gone; it was almost 10:00 a.m. and the serious anglers were finished for the day. He searched for the surveillance boat, but didn't see it. There were no vessels, large or small. Felix focused on the dock and saw the cage in the same spot where the Zodiac had unloaded it two hours ago. The kid, the lizard's guardian that Dedo had told him about, was sitting cross-legged next to it, looking up at the sky. Nothing had changed.

Felix' spirits soared. No one was watching. His fears had been groundless. He started the engine and headed in. He would get his lizard after all. He calculated eight minutes to the dock and a couple more to wrestle the cage onto his boat. In ten minutes, he would be away, heading full speed toward Long Beach with his prize. He hoped the Motagua would thrive in the habitat he had created at his home.

The Cuiza was getting restless. He paced around the dock and stared up at the pale blue sky. What was happening? No one had told him anything. When were they coming back to get him? It was midmorning and he was hungry and thirsty. He had no food, no water, and nothing in his pockets but his lighter. The temperature was rising and the Lizard King, seeking shelter from the sun, had burrowed down under the moss and wood chips.

"Chik, chik, chik." The Cuiza removed his T-shirt and placed it over the top of the cage. *Don't worry Lizard King. I'll take care of you. Nothing will happen to you.*

When he saw the boat approaching, he stood up and walked to the end of the dock.

Felix came in slow and bumped against one of the old tires hanging over the side of the dock. He left the engine running while he jumped off the *Truckin* and secured it with a bowline. His hands were trembling. The cage was only a few feet away. It was bigger than he had expected, and he cursed his son again for not being there to help him.

Felix looked at the kid. His age was uncertain—he looked thin, almost hollowed-out. Felix had seen hundreds just like him on the streets in cities all over Mexico. They lived in the city parks and in abandoned buildings, and all had the same hungry look. He had used boys like this for low-level tasks in his smuggling operations—he liked them because they were expendable, throwaways he didn't have to worry about if something happened to them. At the moment, all he cared about was his lizard. The kid? He could stay on the dock forever.

Felix took a step toward the cage.

The Lizard King's dream-voice told the Cuiza this was a bad man.

"Chik, chik, chik."

The kid made a strange noise. Felix pointed to the cage and said, "*Pertenece a mí*—It belongs to me. The lizard is mine."

The kid stepped between Felix and the lizard.

Felix punched the kid, hit him hard with a direct blow to the cheekbone. The impact knocked the small boy backward onto the dock. Felix followed up with a kick to his ribs and the boy cried out, rolled over on his side, and doubled up in pain. Felix grabbed one end of the cage and began to drag it toward the *Truckin*.

The force of the blow caught the Cuiza by surprise and sent him crashing down. When the man kicked him, he felt the blow through his entire body. He lay dazed for a few seconds, then struggled to his feet. The pain almost took him down again, but he shut it out.

The Lizard King was right; this was a bad man, trying to take him away. *Don't worry—I promised nothing will happen to you. I'll stop him.*

The Cuiza didn't pause. He didn't feel the pain. He had to protect the Lizard King. He put his head down and launched himself. He hit the man in his soft stomach and heard a whoosh as the air rushed out of his lungs. The man dropped the end of the cage and staggered backward off the edge of the dock. When he fell down onto the deck of his boat, his head struck one of the metal rope cleats.

The Cuiza stood and watched the blood begin to leak across the white deck. The man didn't move. The boy untied the boat and shoved it away from the dock with his foot.

"Chik, chik, chik." *We can't stay here.* The Cuiza dragged the cage off the dock and across the gray quartz sand. His face hurt and his ribs screamed with each breath, but nothing could stop him from protecting the Lizard King.

DeAndra leaned over the bathroom sink, splashed cold water on her face, and patted her eyes with a paper towel. She had to get back to her flight console. Emergency breaks without backup were limited to three minutes, and she had already spent almost ten minutes locked in the bathroom. She glanced at her puffy face in the mirror before she unlocked the door. When she returned to her workstation, she saw that the lat-long coordinates for Arizona were flashing on her monitor. She wanted to continue to watch the boy on the dock, but there was no time. She entered the coordinates into the guidance system and the drone began to move east from Catalina Island toward the Arizona border. From two miles up, the camera in the nose sent back a picture of an empty blue sky.

During her lunch break, DeAndra sat in the deserted Customs and Border Patrol commissary in a stupor. She glanced at the clock on the wall. It was only 11:05 a.m., but it seemed like she had been on duty forever. She still had four hours until she completed her shift. She wanted to go home, draw the curtains against the harsh desert sun and hide in bed, but that wasn't an option. At five-o'clock she had a meeting with her son's teachers to discuss why he was doing so poorly in school and fighting with other children. It was important that she arrived looking composed and engaged. She had seven hours to calm down and clear her head. She opened her bottle of Prazosin and dropped a single pink capsule on the dirty table.

When she left Las Vegas and began her new job with Customs and Border Patrol in Riverside, DeAndra transferred to the VA Hospital in Loma Linda, California, where she visited a psychiatrist once every three months for half an hour, just long enough to talk about how she was dealing with her meds. Since coming to California, she had tried Lexapro, Paxil, Zoloft, and then Effexor. At her last meeting, she had complained to her doctor, "The Effexor isn't any better than what I was taking before. I'm not sleeping well and the nightmares are getting worse. There's a young boy chasing me through my dreams. He won't leave me alone. When I'm awake, I feel sad and depressed, and I'm exhausted all the time. Sometimes I break down in tears at work. I've got a twelve-year-old son with his own problems. I'm his mother, I'm supposed to help him—how can I do that when I can't even help myself?"

"We can try one more thing," her psychiatrist had told her. "Prazosin. It may help you for the insomnia and nightmares, but if I start you on it, you have to promise to stay with it for at least three months. You can't come back here in a couple of weeks and tell me it doesn't work. Can you do that?"

"Do I have a choice?"

He wrote a prescription and handed it to her. "You should be aware that it's not FDA-approved for PTSD treatment."

"What does that mean?"

"It was developed to treat high blood pressure, so this is an off-label use, but we've gotten some good results. You may feel dizzy or lightheaded for a few days until your body gets used to it, that's natural. If you find you have a pounding heartbeat, shortness of breath or chest pains after a couple of weeks, then you can call me, otherwise, I don't want to hear from you for three months."

She wasn't supposed to take the Prazosin capsule until noon, but DeAndra popped it into her mouth and washed it down with a sip of her Coke. She stared with disgust at the egg salad sandwich she had purchased and pushed it away.

When she looked up, she saw him. The boy was sitting alone at a table on the far side of the cafeteria. The twelve-year-old from the dock was staring at her. She began to cry.

"Here they come," Ryan said.

"About fucking time," Victor said. He looked at his watch. "It's after noon. Can you believe we've been drifting out here for two and a half hours?"

"Today I can believe anything." Ryan was in a black mood as he looked through his glasses at the Coast Guard Patrol Boat headed toward them. As it approached, Ryan saw that it was towing a small fishing boat. He imagined all the crap he and Victor would take from the Coast Guard men in the task force when they heard what had happened. "You're gonna do what?" he heard them say. "You're gonna follow the drugs? Don't forget to fill your gas tank." Ryan was already gritting his teeth.

When the patrol boat backed down its engines and drifted up near them, Victor waved his badge. "DEA," he yelled.

An ensign came to the railing and hailed them through a megaphone. "Are you the ones who called for help?"

"That's right," Victor shouted, "We're out of gas."

"Hold on," the ensign said. "We'll get you a can of gas."

"Can we come onboard?" Ryan called. "I've got to get off this bathtub for a few minutes. I need to use your john."

"Where are you headed?" the ensign asked.

"The Larson Marina in San Pedro," Victor said. "That's where we rented this piece of junk."

The ensign turned to an officer standing next to him to confer for a moment, and then called back, "We're headed into to San Pedro with an accident victim. How about we just tow your boat in?"

"You don't have to ask twice," Ryan shouted.

While the crew of the patrol boat rigged a towline, Ryan and Victor were helped aboard.

"Executive Petty Officer Owens," a man in a white uniform said, and extended his hand. "Welcome aboard the Coast Guard Cutter Halibut."

Ryan shook his hand. At first glance, the white uniform reminded him of the man who had piloted the Zodiac to the dock at Paradise Cove.

"You the ones who were watching the big yacht?" the petty officer asked.

"Yup," Victor said. "We've spent the last fourteen hours waiting for something that didn't happen. *Nada*."

"One of our cutters is following it back to Mexican waters right now," the petty officer said.

"We were expecting something big," Ryan said. "We had an entire task force geared up to respond to what we thought would be a major drug drop. There's gonna be a lot of disappointed law enforcement people."

"Is that what I think it is?" Victor said, glancing at what appeared to be a body lying on the deck, loosely wrapped in a blue tarp.

"Yeah," the petty officer said. "That's why it took us so long to get to you. We got called out of Marina Del Rey to look for his boat and found him dead, lying on his deck. The Coroner's waiting for us in San Pedro. We left him out here because, after he died, he—uh—he shit his pants."

"What happened?" Victor asked.

"Not sure. Two or three times a year we get a boating casualty, but it's almost always a drowning. I don't ever remember seeing anyone who slipped and cracked open the side of his head on a deck cleat. His boat was drifting in the channel. Some fishermen came alongside, saw him, and called us. It must have happened this morning, because when we lifted him up, rigor mortis hadn't set in." The petty officer pulled back the tarp. "Poor guy. Not the way to end a day of fishing."

Ryan saw a middle-aged man wearing an old shirt, jeans, and deck shoes. His gray hair was matted with dried blood from a nasty gash on the side of his head. Even with the sea wind blowing over the bow of the cutter, a foul smell still hovered around him from the release of his bowels.

"Phew," Victor said.

Ryan held his hand over his mouth and nose and bent closer to the man's face. "I don't believe it. Victor look, do you recognize this guy?"

Victor stared at the dead man's face. "No, who is he?"

"C'mon Victor. Look. It's El Chapo, the head of the Sinaloa Cartel."

"What?" Victor looked again, getting another whiff of the disgusting odor.

"This is incredible," Ryan said. "It's Juaquin Guzman, the kingpin of the Sinaloa Cartel. Wait till the task force hears about this. We've got El Chapo!"

"Oh, bullshit," Victor said. "This guy's too big. El Chapo's a shrimp. This isn't Guzman."

Ryan cackled and broke into a broad grin. "Gotcha."

"Gotcha?" the petty officer said.

"Sorry, just imagining what might have been," Ryan said, backing away from the odor. "I told you, the last few hours have been pretty disappointing."

"Wait, maybe this guy has a cell phone," Victor said. "We could confiscate it and check all his numbers. We could find out who he plays golf with, and go out and harass them."

"You guys need some rest," the petty officer said. "Or maybe some coffee." He pulled the tarp back over the dead man. "Come on into the galley, I'll get you something."

Ryan was at his desk reading about the fire on Catalina Island when he was called in to see the SAC—the Special Agent in Charge. Walking down the hall, he smelled microwave popcorn from the break room. Ryan had a bad feeling—he was rarely called in to a one-on-one meeting with the man who ran the entire Los Angeles Field Division. The door to the SAC's office was ajar and Ryan knocked and walked in.

The SAC didn't smile when he glanced up from the papers he was reading. He said, "Sit down Daniels, I'll be right with you." His voice was gruff.

Ryan sat still, barely breathing the stuffy air in the SAC's office. By DEA standards it was a large space, with several chairs set around a small conference table covered with files. The American and California State flags hung limp in the dead air in one corner of the room. Next to the flags, the seal of the DEA—a large stylized logo of an eagle flying over an earth surrounded by the legend U.S. DEPARTMENT OF JUSTICE DRUG ENFORCEMENT ADMINISTRATION—hung in a cheap frame. Over his boss' left shoulder, Ryan saw two pictures. In the first, the SAC was shaking the President's hand; in the second, he stood in a jungle clearing, surrounded by several men wearing camouflage and holding automatic rifles. On an adjacent wall, a large frame held a wanted poster that offered a $5 million reward for Rafael Caro Quintero, the infamous

Mexican drug trafficker who had tortured and killed a DEA agent and later had walked out of a Mexican jail. While Ryan waited for his boss to stop reading and break the silence, he heard a faint sound of shouting. Even in the SAC's office, he could hear the prisoners across the way at the Metropolitan Detention Center, screaming from their outdoor exercise cage on the fifteenth floor.

"So, Ryan," the SAC finally said, pushing his papers aside.

Ryan looked at his boss' face, trying to get an indication of what was coming. He was scowling.

"I understand the big yacht from Mexico didn't turn out to be what everyone hoped."

"No, sir." Ryan shifted in his chair. "It was a disappointment. A big disappointment, but we—"

"And I heard the Coast Guard found a body on a boat drifting in the San Pedro Channel later that morning?"

"That's right, they—"

"And when they picked you up, you made some kind of bad-ass joke about the body?" He leaned forward and put his hands on his desk. The SAC's brown eyes drilled into Ryan's head. He still wasn't smiling. "Is that right?"

"Yes, I—"

"You said it was Juaquin Guzman?"

"Yes sir."

"Juaquin Guzman? That's who you thought it was? El Chapo? "

"Sir, I—"

"Well, it wasn't Juaquin Guzman." The SAC sat silent and glared at Ryan for a long minute, then broke into a broad grin and slammed his open hand down on his desk. "But damned if it wasn't Felix Cabrera, the boss of the Sinaloa Cartel's cocaine distribution for the entire U.S. Maybe not as important as Guzman, but still, a kingpin in the hierarchy, a big boss." He opened his desk drawer and pulled out a plastic evidence envelope. He slid it across his desk and it fell into Ryan's lap. "And we got his cellphone, which is loaded with numbers. You and Victor are going to be very busy, so get out of my office and go to work."

Ryan exhaled and said, "Thank you, sir."

When he walked out of the SAC's office, Ryan felt lightheaded. He leaned against the wall and closed his eyes for a moment. He was with Sharon. They were on vacation, lying on the beach in Cabo San Lucas.

VI | THE LIZARD

The Motagua Valley beaded lizard's most active period occurs during the wet season, and he may spend a few hours each day outside. The reproduction season begins near the end of the wet season, when his inner clock tells him it is time to mate before moving into a permanent shelter for his dormant period.

Chemical scent cues help him to return to familiar places. Using his tongue, his keen chemosensory system will lead him to a burrow where a female is waiting. Sometimes his quest will cover as much as a half-mile.

Access to a female may first require combat with another lizard, and he sometimes engages in ritual bouts that last half a day. Strength is critical in the battle that begins when he attempts to establish dominance by pressing the head of his opponent to the ground. The opponent will raise his head to counter the effort. They will circle each other until he is able to climb on top of his adversary and grasp its trunk with his legs. Using his strong tail for leverage, the lizard arches his body and leans against his opponent until he can flip him over and bite him. If his rival is able to squirm away, he initiates successive rounds of combat until the other lizard is exhausted and flees.

He carries his own scars where he has been bitten in less successful battles.

Combat with an opponent is a stimulus for copulation. Once the Motagua Valley beaded lizard has forced his adversary to the ground and won access to the female, he enters her shelter and pursues her until he is able to climb up on top of her and rub her head and neck with his chin. Then he grips her with his hind legs and explores her body with his forked tongue. When she becomes receptive, she raises her tail and initiates copulation, which may last for several hours. During this interaction, he gently bites her on the neck and flicks her body with his tongue

When he is finished, the beaded lizard retreats to his own shelter and leaves the female alone to lay four to eight eggs in her underground burrow. The eggs will hatch in four to five months, and the hatchlings may not emerge from the burrow for another five to seven months.

During his dormancy, the lizard will use stored energy in the form of fat in his tail to last through the months of inactivity.

VII | GINA

Gina Winters, Director of Wildlife Management for the Catalina Island Conservancy, selected two grey field mice from the colony she kept in her animal laboratory. She dropped them into a plastic container and went out to the pens at the back of the wood-and-stucco ranch house the Conservancy provided for her living quarters and animal facility. It had been hot most of the day, but a brisk wind off the mainland had come up late in the afternoon and the temperature had dropped. It was a clear, crisp night when she stepped outside. Stars shone in the sky and a new moon reflected a bright sliver of light.

Over the years, Gina had kept specimens of most of the island's wildlife in her cages and pens. Feral cats and pigs, mule deer, desert night lizards, skinks, salamanders and shrews, and even bullfrogs had all been temporary guests. Only the island's bison, which are not indigenous, were too big to be corralled. Tonight everything was empty except a vivarium where she was breeding arboreal salamanders and the outdoor enclosure with the endangered Catalina Island fox. When she turned on the outdoor lights, she saw the animal curled in the far corner, a ball of reddish-grey fur. He uncurled himself, stretched, and came to the wire—still limping slightly on his injured hind leg. Gina gazed at the animal, the size of a small house cat with big ears, a long bushy tail, and wearing a radio-frequency tracking collar. "You hungry?" she said. Gina opened the gate and dangled one of the tiny mice by its tail. The fox snapped it from her fingers, chewing and swallowing in a few seconds. The second mouse met the same fate. Finished, the fox licked his muzzle with a pink tongue and stared expectantly at Gina. "That's enough, old man," she told the animal. "Another week and you'll be good to go. Then you can eat all the mice you can catch." She locked the pen and turned off the lights.

When Gina came around to the side of the house, the wind hit her in the face. She stopped, took a deep breath through her nose, tilted her head up, and took another breath. She caught a trace of smoke and the realization caused goose bumps on her arms. "No," she cried, and ran into the house to get her cellphone. Any fire on Catalina was a threat to the island's fragile ecosystems, and it had taken years for life to stabilize after the island's last blaze in 2007. That fire, the worst in the island's history—started by welders working on a radio tower—had laid waste to most of the east end, and almost forced the evacuation of Avalon, the 100-year-old town that contained most of the island's tiny population. Gina had arrived on Catalina just after that calamity, and her first task had been to assess the damage to the wildlife, especially to the bald eagles and Island Foxes, both of which were on the endangered species list. What Catalina did not need, Gina thought as she turned on her cellphone, was another fire.

She punched the number for the double nickel, Los Angeles County Fire Department Station 55 in Avalon, but disconnected before the first ring. What if Brad answered? She had managed to avoid him for the last six weeks and wasn't anxious to talk to him. She paused for a moment, then dialed again. The fact that there might be a fire trumped her personal problems. Brad might not even be on duty, but if he did pick up, she would be matter of fact and tell him about the smoke.

When the answering machine responded, she was almost relieved. She glanced at her watch. It was 10:45 p.m. Station 55 was staffed with two men, a captain and an engineer, and they had nowhere to go at this hour unless they were responding to an incident. Should she call Station 155 at the other end of the island? It wasn't much more than a large garage, home base for a paramedic and the lifeguards who watched the beaches around Two Harbors, and no one would be there at this hour.

Gina's house was on the edge of the Middle Ranch compound, which included the Conservancy's administration building, a native plant nursery, facilities maintenance, and housing for the rangers and other employees. From her kitchen, she could see the glow in the windows from the lights in their bunkhouse and when she called, Cole, one of the rangers, answered on the first ring.

"Hi Gina," he said. "Yes. The answer is yes."

"Yes, what?"

"Yes, there's a fire. It started somewhere above Paradise Cove."

"I knew I smelled smoke. How bad is it?"

"Can't tell. County Fire's out there right now, and they've called for help from the Conservancy. I was just about out the door when you called."

"Paradise Cove? How did it start?"

"I dunno. Sorry, I can't stop to talk, I've got to go."

Gina asked, "Should I head over there?" but Cole had already hung up. "Damn right I should," she said aloud. She threw on a jacket, grabbed the keys to her pickup, and ran outside.

Her relationship with Brad might be over, but during their affair Gina had learned a lot from him about firefighting on Catalina. The island, twenty-two miles long and eight miles wide, lay twenty-five miles southwest of Los Angeles. Rocky mountains dotted the rugged landscape and steep canyons ran up from remote beaches of grey quartz.

There were few paved roads outside of Avalon, the use of motor vehicles was restricted, and getting fire engines and tank trucks to the site of a blaze was a difficult, sometimes impossible task. Most of the island was covered with Eucalyptus and oak trees, chaparral, coastal sage and manzanita, and patches of thick grasses, all of which thrived in the semi-arid climate and all of which made perfect tinder for a wildfire; eucalyptus trees in particular acted like torches and burned with intensity. And there was no natural supply of water anywhere on Catalina—the populace drank from a small desalinization plant and a separate sewage system used seawater. Worst of all, in an emergency the island could only field about three dozen firefighters—a few professionals from Station 55 and the volunteers who trained on Tuesday nights. A significant blaze would quickly overwhelm them and if the fire picked up any momentum, firefighters and equipment would have to come over from the mainland. That would take hours. How had a fire started in Paradise Cove? The weather was clear, so lightning couldn't be the cause, and camping in that area was forbidden. It seemed such an unlikely place for a fire. She was particularly concerned because one of the few bald eagle nesting sites—a spot where two eggs had hatched the previous year—was nearby.

As Gina drove down Middle Ranch Road in the old F-150 that belonged to the Conservancy, the smell of wood smoke became stronger. The Conservancy compound was near the center of the island and the cove, directly north, was only five miles away. The problem was that the terrain in between was rocky and mountainous, and there was no direct route. There were only a few roads that crisscrossed the island and even the most direct route would take Gina more than three miles west on Middle Ranch Road, then north on Isthmus Road for almost two miles, and finally east, up Sheep Chute Road for approximately five miles. Middle Ranch and Isthmus were one-lane, hard-packed dirt roads; Sheep Chute was what the Conservancy referred to as a mid-slope, secondary road.

That meant it was not much more than a wide trail. It was winding, steep in places, with spots covered with scree and shale that had tumbled down from the surrounding hillsides. In the middle of the night, with only the weak headlights from her old pickup, the ten-mile drive would take Gina close to an hour and would bring her out on a ridge high above the beach at Paradise Cove.

Creeping along the dark road, Gina remembered the day of her interview years ago. When she drove around the seventy-six square mile island with a Conservancy Ranger, she discovered that Catalina was as arid as her childhood home in Phoenix. She'd grown up in a suburb on the edge of the desert, and had been fascinated with animals, especially reptiles, as far back as she could remember. While other girls played with dolls, Gina brought home injured snakes and lizards. After graduating from the University of Arizona with a B.S. in Zoology, she had high hopes, but struggled to find a job.

"A degree in zoology?" her father had said. "What can you do with that?"

"I want to work with animals," Gina had insisted, but secretly feared she might end up working at a Pet Smart. Months later, out of desperation, she accepted the only job offer she had and went to work for the Law Enforcement Division of the U.S. Fish and Wildlife Service. They sent her to Miami, the entry portal for all the endangered species coming out of Latin America.

Gina's job was to investigate illegal trafficking, a huge business, and she soon learned how futile it was to go after reptile smugglers. For every shipment she stopped, for every illegal importer she found with forged paperwork and rare snakes or lizards in shipping cases, dozens more evaded detection. The creatures themselves were hardy and easy to transport—just lower their temperature and they didn't even move— and the smugglers made huge profits with little risk. They weren't dealing in weapons or drugs where the danger and up-front expense could be huge. Moreover, they didn't have to contend with any of the tough federal law-enforcement agencies like the DEA, the ATF, or the FBI. All they had to face was the under-staffed, under-funded Fish and Wildlife Service. The offenders Gina caught were rarely convicted and if they were, they served a few months in prison, only to be released to make room for those who had committed more important crimes. After almost a decade on the job, Gina was completely demoralized. She had decided that trying to curb the international trade in imperiled species was hopeless—most people would simply grab a shovel and kill the very creatures she was struggling to protect. She was sick of the long hours, the lousy government pay scale, and the rain and humidity in South Florida. When the offer came from the Catalina Island Conservancy, she didn't think twice about accepting it.

In 1972, the descendants of William Wrigley, Jr.—the chewing gum magnate had purchased the island in 1919—deeded most of Catalina to the Conservancy, which was created to manage and support programs to protect the island's plant and animal species, many of which existed nowhere else in the world. When Gina arrived, she embraced her job with enthusiasm. For the first time since graduating college, she felt she was actually helping endangered animals instead of chasing after scumbag smugglers. The only downside to Catalina was that Gina missed South Florida's endless supply of good-looking Latin men. Miami, filled with clubs and sidewalk cafes open late into the night, attracted a young, vibrant crowd of people intent on having a good time. Gina wasn't a great beauty, but she was decent looking, with an assertive personality and an appetite for sex that attracted men. She wished she were taller, and her legs were thinner, but her breasts were ample and that was what men really cared about. During the years she worked for Fish and Game, she was never without a male companion, and when she became tired of the one sharing her bed, she ousted him and found someone new. Catalina was another story—it was a social wasteland. There were only 3,000 residents on the entire island, and most of the male residents were old, with big bellies and unkempt beards. Although almost a million tourists visited the island each year during the summer, the majority arrived on the ferry in the morning, walked around Avalon's waterfront, and left in the evening.

Gina wasn't looking for a husband—she was far too independent to let a man run her life—but she needed male companionship. After coming to Catalina, she spent a lot of time alone until she met Brad, a captain with the Los Angeles County Fire Department. He worked at Station 55, and was big, strong, and good-looking. All her Latin lovers had been dark and she was attracted to his blond hair. She loved running her fingers over the blond carpet that covered his chest. At thirty-six, he was five years younger than she was, and married. Brad was perfect.

Their affair lasted almost two years. She didn't see him every day—in fact, she didn't *want* to see him every day. His wife and daughter lived in Seal Beach, and once a week he took the ferry to the mainland and spent three days at home. But he didn't always head home right away, and they often stole a few hours together on one of the remote beaches on the rugged, wind-swept west end of the island. During the off-season, they sometimes managed to spend a night at a local bed and breakfast in Avalon, and occasionally she cooked dinner for him at the ranch house. When nothing else worked, they drove up into the hills and screwed in the back of his SUV. For Gina it was a perfect relationship—she got what she needed without making a major emotional commitment.

Her relationship with Brad had gone on longer than any other liaison she had ever had and she'd begun to wonder how long it could last. She found out six weeks ago when they had lunch together in Avalon at a Mexican restaurant. Pancho's was a tiny place on a street that dead-ended at the water. It was sandwiched between a boatyard and the paved landing pad Brad referred to as Helispot 55A, where fire helicopters came in from the mainland. They sat outside on cement benches around a table with a Corona Beer umbrella. The early-afternoon sun hung bright in a pale blue sky, the Pacific Ocean crashed against the jetty at the boatyard, and the cries of gulls filled the air while they fought for scraps around the trashcans. Gina sensed something was wrong and watched Brad push a burrito around his plate with a fork. When he finally looked at her, his eyes were troubled.

"Are you okay?" she asked. "What's the matter?"

"It's over," he said. "My wife's leaving me. It's not working. Things have been lousy for a long time and we've decided to call it quits."

Gina was aware that he had been having marital problems, but he'd never told her how serious it was. "I'm sorry," she said in a flat voice. She knew what was coming next and didn't want to hear it.

"You and I," he began. "Maybe we could—"

"No Brad," she interrupted. "We couldn't." She had to stop that conversation before he started it.

He rubbed his eyes and looked at her. "Gina, I love you, and—"

"No," she said. "No, you don't love me. You may think you do now, but you don't. That was part of our understanding. Remember? We weren't going to fall in love." They stared at each other for a moment before she repeated, "Brad, you *do not* love me." It was nonnegotiable. Gina had tried to sound resolute and adamant. Before he could say another word, she had jumped up and gone out to her pickup, leaving him alone with a plate of half-eaten food.

For days afterward, he called and sent text messages, but she ignored him. What was Brad thinking? He was a fool if he had broken up his marriage for her. She had no interest in spending the rest of her life with him. Didn't he understand that? She had never, ever told him she loved him, and had never encouraged him to believe that she did. Their relationship was physical, no more, and now there was nothing for them to discuss. It was an affair. It was fun while it lasted, and it was over. She would miss Brad, but she was also upset because now she had to find another man and that wasn't going to be easy on Catalina Island.

Six weeks had passed and they hadn't spoken. As Gina drove through the darkness toward the fire, she knew she would see Brad before the night was over.

Brad Stillman stood next to his four-wheel-drive Suburban on the ridge above Paradise Cove, giving Chief Turner at Battalion 14 on the mainland a size-up over the radio. "We've got an interior fire over here, burning toward the center of the island. It's consumed maybe ten acres, but the wind's coming up now and it's going to spread fast. I'm requesting a full brushfire response." Because he was first on the scene and the acting incident commander, it was Brad's responsibility to name the fire. "We'll call this the Paradise Fire," he told the chief.

Brad wasn't a stranger to fighting brushfires, but this was the first serious one he'd faced on Catalina. The only equipment at Station 55 was a heavy-duty brushfire rig and a water tender. Using the rig, he could knock down something small with the help of his engineer and the small number of trained volunteers and Conservancy rangers, but it was too late to contain the Paradise Fire to a few acres. He watched the flames burn through a large patch of dry vegetation, moving toward a stand of oak trees, and saw the beginning of a major incident. It was only May, but Southern California was in its fourth year of drought and after another dry winter and spring, the moisture level in the trees and brush was already down to levels usually seen only in August and September.

The Los Angeles County Fire Department had a thirty-two-page protocol for responding to wildland incidents on the island—they called it the Catalina Plan—and Brad had it memorized. It detailed every step in a complicated procedure and he had just taken the first step by calling for a brushfire response. Now that the request had been made, a cascade of events would be set in motion, but it would take time. Brad needed strike teams, wildland crews, and air tankers, and he needed them at once, but the logistics were a nightmare. Everything had to come over from the mainland.

The wind was blowing south and Brad knew where the fire was headed. "I expect it will make a run toward the airport before daylight," he told the chief. "We have to get the camp crews over there to start cutting line as soon as possible." He had already dispatched the brushfire rig along with a dozen volunteers to start hacking a three-foot wide firebreak, but they were slow and inexperienced and could do little to protect the buildings and aircraft. Fortunately, Air Ops could dispatch wildland hand crews in helicopters, even in the dark. Now that County Fire had begun flying with night vision equipment, the Firehawks—Blackhawk attack helicopters modified for firefighting—would be taking off within minutes after Brad's call, each carrying a fourteen-man crew with Pulaskis, chainsaws, and shovels. "Notify me when the birds are in the air," he said to his chief. Brad hoped he would be able to save the airport with the help of the wildland crews, but regardless, the head of fire would continue to burn uncontested for several more hours until a coordinated defense could be mounted. "It'll probably move toward the center of the island and hit the Conservancy facilities at Middle Ranch sometime tomorrow morning," he said. "We'll have to make a stand there."

As part of the response, engines, crews, and equipment would stage at the Catalina Island Freight dock on the mainland before there was light in the morning sky and load onto barges for the two-hour trip across to the island. "The barges should unload at the freight ramp in

Avalon, and it's about a six-mile trip on dirt roads to Middle Ranch," he advised his chief. "I'm going to head over to the airport now and organize the hand crews. I'll be at the ramp to meet you by the time the barges get here in the morning." Once full daylight arrived, Brad would have another weapon: aerial bombardment. The same Firehawks that were bringing in the camp crews also carried water tanks on their bellies. Using snorkels that dangled from the aircraft, they could hover, pick up water, and make strategic drops. He could also call in the fixed-wing air tankers, the Super Scoopers, that could suck up seawater on the fly and drop it almost anywhere. Support from the air was critical, but it couldn't be done in the dark.

Brad watched as the fire continued to advance, creeping across the ridge and beginning to burn down into one of the neighboring canyons. Before he signed off, he told the chief, "We also need an arson investigator over here in the morning; this has to be a human-caused fire."

Catalina wasn't exactly action-central and for the first time in months, Brad felt the rush of adrenaline fed by the excitement and danger of a major wildfire.

He had been a rising star within the fire department, progressing in almost record time from boot firefighter to paramedic, then engineer, and finally promoting to captain. Unfortunately, as Brad rose through the ranks, both his marriage and his relationship with his daughter suffered—he and his wife Ann had somehow reached a point where they spent most of their time arguing, and his nine-year old daughter seemed to regard him as a total stranger. Brad had requested the assignment on Catalina because the duty wasn't as demanding, his intervals at home would be longer, and he thought it would give him the time to get his marriage back on track. But things had gotten worse. His marriage had turned to quicksand and he felt himself being sucked inexorably down.

The more he struggled, the deeper he sank. Each week he sat on the Catalina Express and watched happy couples holding hands and kissing while the huge, high-speed ferry slapped across the water toward Long Beach. He tried to remember when he and Ann had been that happy, but it seemed like some other lifetime. Each time he arrived home, she was angrier and more combative. He thought he still loved her, but his emotions were muddled by his affair with Gina. They had been seeing each other for almost two years. At first, it was a casual relationship, a temporary diversion from his difficulties at home. But the worse things became with Ann, the more he depended on seeing Gina.

Finally, he and his wife decided to call it quits. Their daughter was the only thing left that they shared—everything else between them seemed to have evaporated. When he left his house, Ann stood on the driveway and cried, "Don't come back here. I don't want to see you again—stay over there on that damn island!" He had returned to Catalina and sat on the tiny porch at the back of Station 55 at dusk, listening to the wind blowing through the palm trees that lined the street. He was devastated at the thought of what would happen to his already frayed relationship with his daughter. He felt empty and alone and his thoughts turned to Gina. He wanted to see her, talk to her, be with her. He needed the comfort of feeling her next to him. . He wanted to make love to her.

The following day, he called Gina and asked her to join him at the small Mexican food place near the helipad. He had no appetite, only a knot in his stomach. They made small talk for a few moments while she ate her lunch and he tried to decide how to begin the real conversation. He'd been awake all night and his mind was fuzzy. He had planned in detail what he wanted to tell her, but sitting across from her in the bright daylight, he forgot everything. Finally, he just blurted out, "It's over. My wife is leaving me. It's not working and we've decided to call it quits."

He searched her face for some indication of her feelings, some hint of understanding. She gave him nothing; she was impassive and silent. "You and I," he said in a low, tentative voice. "Maybe we could—"

Gina interrupted. "No Brad, we couldn't."

Her tone was so matter of fact, so hard, that he was stunned. There was no hint of the kindness and solace he desperately needed. After all the shared meals and conversations, the jokes, the stories—and, most important, after the countless hours of making love—all she could say was *no*? That was it? No? At this moment, he questioned whether he even knew the woman sitting across from him, just as he had wondered if he had really known the woman in Seal Beach to whom he had been married for so many years. He waited for encouragement, empathy, anything, but nothing came. Finally, his emotions churning, he uttered the words he had promised himself he wouldn't say. "I think I'm in love with you."

He saw her brow furrow and her jaw tighten before she said, "No, you don't love me. I won't let you. That was never part of our arrangement." She leaned forward, looked him in the eye and repeated, "You *do not* love me."

The rest of the conversation Brad imagined they would have, about their feelings for each other, and about the plans they might make together, never happened. Without saying another word, Gina stood up, walked away from the table and away from their relationship.

That was the end of it.

He tried to reach her, but hadn't heard back from her or even seen her since that conversation at the taco joint. Considering how small the island was, he knew she was going out of her way to avoid him. He was left to ponder how someone who cared so much about animals could be so indifferent to another person's feelings.

Brad ended the conversation with Chief Turner and watched the flames advancing across the ridge. Fire was a huge threat to the island's wildlife and Gina's job was to protect the animals. He was certain she would come out to check on the situation.

As Gina crested the ridge in her pickup, the orange glow of the fire became brighter and the smell of smoke more intense. She drove around a bend on Sheep Chute and saw flashing red and orange lights. When she pulled abreast of Brad's Suburban, she saw him standing by the open driver's side door, holding a radio. He looked up and nodded.

"How bad is it?" she asked through her open window.

"Hey, Gina." He stared at her for a moment. "It's spreading. I've called for a full response from the mainland."

"Can I drive on a little farther? There's a bald eagle habitat up here. I have to see if it's threatened."

"I wouldn't. It's dangerous and there's nothing you can do. You won't see anything in the dark anyway."

"I still want to take a look."

He shrugged his shoulders. "Close your windows and stay in the truck. Don't get too close. The flames can move fast, so stop where you can turn around, in case the fire starts to make a run."

Before Gina could close her window, he stepped closer, put his hand on her door, and bent to look in at her. She saw Brad the fire captain, not the wounded man at the Mexican restaurant who had been agonizing over his marriage. He looked very handsome and rugged.

"Be careful," he said. "Come right back."

Gina's heart was pounding as she drove slowly across the ridge— she wasn't certain whether it was because she'd just seen Brad for the first time in six weeks, or because she was a half mile away from a ferocious fire. The flames were deep orange, perhaps thirty feet high, and cast a golden glow into the night sky as they devoured brush and trees. Somewhere below, the beach at Paradise Cove lay in darkness, but the fire illuminated the upper part of the canyon and Gina could see where it had marched uphill. She had watched countless reports of brushfires on television, but seeing one in person was a mesmerizing sight. The fire was a wall of flame moving toward her across the ridge, like a living, breathing creature, consuming everything in its path. If it were really alive, she wondered, what kind of animal would it be? It certainly wasn't a cold-blooded reptile—this monster was all heat, and she felt it on her skin as the wind blew hot, smoky air into the truck.

One afternoon a month earlier, she and Brad lay wrapped in a blanket on an east-facing beach, watching a column of brown smoke from a fire in the Angeles National Forest, rising thousands of feet into the sky over Los Angeles County.

"That's a convection column from the Station Fire," he had told her.

"A convection column?"

"A smoke plume," he said. "A forest fire creates its own weather. Fire needs oxygen, and the hotter it burns, the more oxygen it uses. When you have a really big fire, hot air gets sucked in and rises into a plume, which creates a vacuum at the base that pulls in more air. You can end up with a firestorm, burning at maybe 2,000 degrees and creating hundred mile-an-hour winds. Animals get trapped in those big fires all the time."

He had started to tell her some of the things he had seen, and she'd held her hands over her ears. "No, please, don't tell me."

Gina slowed the pickup to a crawl—she was as close to the fire dragon as she wanted to be—and stopped near a patch of manzanita. She took a flashlight from the back of her truck, hoping she could spot the bald eagle nest. She tried to identify trees, landmarks, anything that was familiar, but it was hopeless. Ahead of her, everything was burning; behind her, everything was dark. She prayed the eagle's nest was safe, knew in her heart that it probably was not, and gave up trying to locate it. This fire would threaten all the animals on the island, including the foxes, which were slowly making a comeback after the last inferno. Also at risk was a rare plant species—the Catalina Mahogany, a plant in the rose family that grows nowhere else on the planet.

When she walked around the pickup and glanced back at the flashing lights of Brad's vehicle, a sound from the nearby brush surprised her.

The Cuiza was in physical and mental agony. His face hurt and his injured ribs sent a sharp pain through his body each time he took a breath. Why? Why had they left him on the island? Why didn't they come back for him? He had trusted Maria Gabriela and she had abandoned him. After the dockside clash with the man who tried to take the Lizard King, the Cuiza realized the big yacht wasn't coming back. He was on his own. He pulled the heavy cage off the dock and began to drag it across the gray sand.

We can't stay here, Lizard King. I'll find someone who will help us.

He started to haul the cage up through the canyon.

By late afternoon, the Cuiza was exhausted and his hands were bloody, the flesh of his fingers torn from grasping the rough wire while dragging the cage. He had lost first one sandal and then the other as he struggled up the hillside. The sun had been hot and he had stopped many times. As the climb up to the ridge had become steeper, his rest periods became longer. When he finally reached the top, he collapsed. The Cuiza was spent. His ribs ached and his cheek throbbed. He hadn't eaten or had anything to drink since leaving the yacht early in the morning. From his vantage point, he looked out over an empty blue-green ocean. A line of white foam formed, disappeared, and formed again where the waves broke on the beach. The dock appeared small and insignificant from the top of the canyon.

The Cuiza had never felt so sad and lonely. He was accustomed to fending for himself and could make his way on the streets in Mexico, but this was different. He knew nothing about survival on an island in a foreign country. He longed for his *mamá* as never before. He still remembered the lemon fragrance of her soft skin when she hugged him to her breast. When he thought of his mother, he also thought of the man who had killed her, and the little gecko he had caught on the cement floor under her bed.

He turned to the Lizard King in the cage. *I promised. I will take care of you.*

The day was finished and still the Cuiza had not moved from his spot on the ridge. After sunset, a wind had come up and the temperature began to drop. His thin cotton pants and T-shirt were not enough to keep him warm, and he began to shiver as darkness descended. He opened the cage, bent his head to the lizard's eye level, and reached in to touch his knobby back. The Cuiza felt the warm, glowing sensation pulse through his body.

Yes, I'll start a fire.

He gathered a small pile of dead brush, leaves, and withered grass, and lit it with his lighter. The heat from the tiny fire warmed and relaxed the Cuiza and he sank into a daze. Through half-closed eyes, he watched the flames, only a few inches high, and when he dozed, the fire crept away. The wind caught the flames and pushed them into the nearby brush. He awoke to a crackling sound and the smell of smoke. The blaze grew higher and ignited the surrounding vegetation.

The Cuiza stood up and began to drag the cage away from the heat and flames, but he was exhausted, he had no strength, and now the fire seemed to be everywhere. He had nowhere to go. The safety of the Lizard King came before all else.

Save yourself Lizard King, save yourself.

He opened the door of the cage, but the Lizard King didn't move.

Go, Lizard King, go!

He managed to pull the cage a little farther, and then slumped down. Just as the Cuiza was certain the flames would consume them both, the wind shifted slightly and the fire moved off in another direction. The heat had sucked away the last drops of moisture from his body. The Cuiza's mouth was dry. He had no spit. He would die without water.

The reassuring dream-voice of the Lizard King spoke: *Todo va bien*— everything will be alright, and at that moment, he saw the pickup truck. A *gringa* got out, holding a flashlight.

"Chik, chik, chik."

Gina paused. What was that? It sounded like the chirping noise geckos made, but geckos were tiny and you had to have your ear right next to one of the little creatures to hear it. This was as loud as a human voice.

"Chik, chik, chik."

Standing in the fire's radiant heat, Gina felt a momentary chill. She held her breath, cupped her ear with one hand to block out the din of the conflagration and listened. She pointed her light into the dense rush and waded through the twisting, waist high foliage toward the spot where she had heard the sound.

"Chik, chik, chik."

Gina was astonished at what she saw in the beam of her flashlight. In an open space, a young boy sat on the ground, one arm resting on a wire animal cage. He had dark skin and his dirty face was streaked with sweat, or perhaps tears. His clothes were filthy and torn, and his feet were bare and bloodied.

When he saw her, he stood up and moved between her and the cage. "Chik, chik, chik."

Gina was stunned to hear him make the sound of a gecko. "Don't be afraid," she told him. "I won't hurt you." She stepped toward him, flashing the light in his face. "My God, where did you come from? What's your name?"

He remained silent and motionless. His brown eyes were wide with terror.

"*Habla Espanol?*" she asked him. By the time she left Miami, Gina had learned to speak almost fluent Spanish, although with a Cuban accent.

The boy continued to stare.

"*Comprende?*" she said, and stepped closer. *Comprende?*"

He gave a tiny nod with his head.

Did he have a name? "*Cómo te llamas?*"

"Chik, chik, chik."

She bent down and pointed her light into the cage. In the moss and wood chips, she saw a partly hidden lizard. It looked like a Gila Monster, a venomous lizard prevalent throughout the southwestern United States and first discovered near the Gila River watershed in her home state of Arizona. She looked around and saw that the fire was edging closer.

"Come on," she said to the boy. When he didn't move, she shouted, "*Vamanos.*" Gina grasped one end of the cage and began to drag it through the brush to her pickup. She was surprised at how heavy it was and when she tried to lift it onto the bed of the truck, she barely got it off the ground. "Help me," she said to the boy, and pointed to the cage. Together they managed to lift the cage up onto the tailgate of the pickup and push it onto the bed. "Get in," she said. She opened the passenger side door and shoved him up onto the seat.

Gina watched the advancing flames out of the corner of her eye and somehow managed to turn the pickup around without going over the side. She started back across the ridge toward Sheep Chute Road and saw Brad, still speaking into his radio. He stepped out into the headlights of her pickup as if to talk to her. Gina swerved around him and kept her foot on the gas pedal.

By the time she returned to Middle Ranch, it was almost 1:30 a.m. With the help of the boy, Gina unloaded the lizard and deposited it, still in its cage, in one of the animal pens. After he bent down and uttered the chirping sound, the boy followed her into the house. Once inside, in her kitchen, he went to the sink, put his mouth under the tap, and drank for several seconds. He choked, coughed, spit water, and drank again.

Gina saw that his hands were raw and torn, and his bare feet had left blood spots on the floor. "You're a mess," she said and pulled him into her bathroom. She turned on the shower, threw a towel across the top of the sink, and told him, "Clean yourself up."

In her bedroom, Gina searched for something he could wear. She was not a large woman, but didn't have much in her wardrobe that would fit the boy. She pulled out an old pair of shorts, a belt, and a T-shirt, tossed them into the bathroom, and closed the door.

When the boy came into the kitchen, Gina saw that the shorts almost fit him, although the T-shirt hung loose on his thin upper body. Now that he was clean and she got a better look at him in the light, Gina saw dark hair, dark eyes, and fine features. When he grew older, he would be handsome.

"*Tienes hambre?*" she asked him. "Are you hungry?"

He nodded.

She pointed to a plate on her small kitchen table with two hamburger patties on buns, a pile of potato chips, and a banana. "Sorry, that's all I've got," she said, and pushed him onto a chair. "I wasn't expecting to cook dinner at this hour." She opened a Coke and slid it across the table.

Gina sat down with him, and he hunched over his plate. While she sipped a cup of lemon Verbena herbal tea, she watched the boy stuff food into his mouth using both hands, and before she finished her tea, he had consumed his meal. She gave him a half-bag of stale chocolate chip cookies and another Coke. He consumed the cookies, drank half the Coke without pausing, and finally came up for air.

The Cuiza leaned back in the kitchen chair and felt the food and cola spilling into his empty stomach. He was exhausted and a peaceful, contented feeling began to creep over him. When the *gringa* sat back down at the table with her cup, he inhaled the lemon aroma from her tea. This special scent brought a flood of forgotten memories of his *mamá*: she leaned over his bed to tuck him in; she tied his shoes before taking him outside; she kissed his finger after he touched a cactus. Then came the clearest image of all, the one he would never forget. The Cuiza saw his mother lying motionless on the floor of the bedroom. The blood leaking from her face made a small, dark-red puddle on the cement. Sitting in the *gringa's* kitchen, the Cuiza wanted his mother. He wanted to touch her—wanted to tell her how much he missed her.

"*Mamá*," he murmured.

"What?" Gina said. "What did you say?"

"*Mamá*," he repeated in a tiny voice.

"Mama? No, I'm not your mother."

The Cuiza felt tired, very tired. His eyelids drooped.

Gina saw his head nod, and led him to the couch in the living room. He was asleep before his head touched the cushions. "Sleep, lizard boy," she said. She threw a sheet over him, turned off the light, and walked back into the kitchen.

Late as it was, Gina was wide-awake. She was worried about the fire. The flames would do huge damage and she wondered how long it would take the firefighters to contain the inferno. She feared for the Island's wildlife; the eagles, the kit foxes, and so many other creatures were all at risk. Gina had no idea how she would even determine the damage to the Bald Eagles—it might take a year or more to just to try to locate and count them. At least each fox wore a radio frequency collar, and if the animal stopped moving for more than twelve hours, the collar would emit an alert signal. She would have to organize an aerial survey as soon as possible to determine how many had perished. The problem was, she realized, if one of the poor creatures had burned to death, the collar would be gone and there would be no signal.

Gina was also worried about her house and the other Conservancy buildings at Middle Ranch. Would tomorrow bring an evacuation? Could the entire facility burn to the ground? How had this fire begun? Was it the boy? It couldn't be just a coincidence that he was at the top of the ridge near the spot where the fire had started. Finally, she pondered the biggest question of all—where had this strange boy come from, and how did he get up there with a Gila Monster in a cage that was almost too heavy to lift?

Something bothered Gina about the lizard—she needed another look at it. She took a flashlight and stopped in her lab to grab a tiny field mouse. Outside, she squatted down by the cage and stared at the reptile in the glow of her light. When she dangled the terrified mouse through the wire, the lizard used its forked tongue to smell it, then lifted itself up by its front legs and closed its jaws around the helpless creature. Gina watched the lizard devour the mouse and her suspicion was confirmed—this reptile was too big to be a Gila Monster; it had to be a Mexican beaded lizard, another member of the small Heloderma family of venomous lizards with skin made of bony, beadlike studs. Studying these unique reptiles years ago in school, she had been fascinated. They traced their existence back to the time of dinosaurs and other creatures that had long since become extinct or had evolved into something else. Only the Helodermatidae family of lizards had remained unchanged after millions of years. Where did this boy get this beaded lizard? They were an endangered and protected species.

Gina returned to the house and went to her computer to search for pictures of Mexican beaded lizards. She brought up several pages, all showing the creatures with pink forked tongues and black bumpy skin. As she began to sort through them, she found images of another beaded lizard, one she hadn't considered because there were so few of them—the Motagua Valley beaded lizard from Guatemala. She clicked back and forth, studying the pale yellow and cream-colored spots and bands on the tails. "Is it possible?" she uttered, and ran out to look at the lizard once more. When she shined her light on the cage again, the lizard was motionless, still ingesting its meal. Gina looked closely at the reptile's tail and drew in a sharp breath. The black and yellow bands in the lizard's tail were very distinct. Each yellow band had a sharply contrasting black band dividing it. The banding on the Mexican beaded lizards in the pictures was not nearly as distinct and clear. Gina was certain—she was looking at a Motagua Valley beaded lizard, one of the rarest reptiles on earth.

Back in the house, Gina's hands shook as she googled the *Convention on International Trade in Endangered Species of Wild Fauna and Flora* and found the Guatemalan lizard listed in Appendix II: *Motagua Valley subspecies (H. charlesbogerti) is one of the rarest lizards in the world, with a wild population of fewer than 200.* Gina sat at her desk, stunned. Once again she wondered how the boy had come to possess such a rare lizard. There were fewer than 200, and he was dragging one around in a cage on Catalina Island?

Her first reaction was that she might keep the rare creature. After a moment, she realized it wasn't possible. Someone would eventually discover it, and how could she ever explain having it? It was an endangered and protected lizard and there was the Lacey Act, which she had spent ten years trying to enforce. Lacey made it a federal crime to possess protected wildlife, and Gina had no intention of violating Federal law and committing a felony by keeping it. The only real question was, what should she do with the lizard? It wouldn't be easy to even give it away. What zoo or wildlife refuge would take it without documentation? She couldn't just call someone and say, "I've got a nearly extinct lizard in a pen at the back of my house, come get it." Who would believe she had found it in a cage, along with a strange boy during a brushfire on Catalina Island? It would create a quicksand of endless, unanswerable questions and she would be suspected in some way of dealing in endangered species. That kind of innuendo might even threaten her position with the Conservancy and damage her entire career.

There was another alternative. All the big drug dealers and cartel bosses were animal collectors. They wanted anything exotic, even reptiles, and the Motagua Valley beaded lizard would be a great prize, an exceptional addition to someone's menagerie. Gina was familiar with the huge black market for endangered species—it had been her job to try to foil it. She was certain the creature out in the pen would be worth an enormous amount to the right customer—money meant nothing to the drug lords. At Fish and Wildlife, she had learned about the underground websites on the dark Internet that offered pornography, weapons, drugs, exotic and endangered species, even forbidden animal parts such as rhino horns, elephant ivory, and bear paws. If she advertised the animal for sale, how high would the bidding go? A million dollars? More? Her mind ran wild. What could she do with $1 million? What *couldn't* she do with $1 million? For a few minutes, Gina was lost in a reverie about all the ways she could spend the money. But she couldn't do it. Her entire purpose in life was to protect endangered creatures like the beaded lizard, not offer them up on the black market. As much as she would like to bank a huge sum of money, selling the lizard was not something Gina Winters would ever allow herself to do.

Once she ruled out selling the reptile, the only other solution was to call Richard, an erstwhile lover she had met years ago while working for Fish and Wildlife. At the time, he was an assistant professor at the University of California at Santa Barbara, and had come to Florida for a month to teach a class about reptiles at University of Miami. They became friendly, he pursued her, and before he went back to California, they had a brief fling. After returning to Santa Barbara, he called her several times, but she never responded. He was a smart man, and had forgotten more about reptiles than she had ever learned, but Gina found him unimaginative and boring—especially in bed. She hadn't spoken with him in years, but knew that he had gone on to establish the Santa Barbara Reptile Institute, an organization that worked as an intermediary to obtain reptiles and other exotic animals for zoos, museums, wealthy collectors, and research institutions. Richard could figure out a way to document the creature and find it a suitable home where it would be safe. She wasn't sure how happy he would be to hear from her after all these years, but was certain he would listen when she told him why she was calling.

Now that Gina had determined the lizard's fate, she had to decide what to do with the boy sleeping on her couch. She had never desired a child of her own and didn't want a strange kid in her house longer than necessary. She guessed he was an undocumented alien and decided to notify the Sheriff's Department as soon as the fire emergency was over. Gina made another cup of tea and sat down at the kitchen table. Thoughts of the fire, the boy, and the lizard swirled through her mind. When she put her head down on the kitchen table, she fell into a deep sleep.

At 2:10 a.m., the tones sounded at Camp 8, reverberating through the sleeping quarters. Before they were even fully awake, three dozen wildland firefighters rolled out of bed, donned their Nomex brush gear, and ran out to the equipment bay to pick up their packs and tools. By the time Crew 1 got to the landing pad, the pilot had already started the engine. The high-pitched whine of the big helicopter's twin turbines filled the night air as the men loaded their gear, and squeezed into the jump seats. The Firehawk lifted off the cement in the Malibu hills and headed out over the dark Pacific toward Catalina, the body of every firefighter on the bird vibrating with energy.

As far back as he could remember, Chris Martinez' father had talked about wildland firefighting and told anyone who would listen that he hoped his son would follow in his footsteps. Chris had honored his father's wishes, and was heading into his first battle against the red devil as the newest member of Air Attack Crew 1. He inhaled the faint smell of hydraulic oil, slipped on his headset, and listened to the chatter between Air Ops and the battalion chief who was acting as incident commander. Chris looked at the faces of the men sitting in the cramped seats across from him and saw anticipation and excitement. Every man on the helicopter lived for the adrenaline spike brought on by battling a big wildfire, even in the deepest hour of the night.

"Your fire crew will be like your family," his father had once told him. "When you're out there on the fire line, those men will watch your back—they'll protect you, even risk their lives to save you. And you'll do the same for them—without even thinking about it—because they're your brothers."

Weeks earlier, Chris had graduated the wildland fire academy run by Los Angeles County Fire Department. *Survived* might have been a better word. Of the twenty-nine men who started, only thirteen had lasted long enough to finish the training. Chris had been in the Army for two years and had seen combat in Iraq, and that experience had been good preparation for the physical and mental demands of the wildland camp. It went on 24/7, and when he wasn't doing endless pushups, running up hillsides with a fifty-pound pack, or learning to cut a three-foot-wide firebreak through thick, shoulder-high brush, he was attending classes to learn about wildland fire behavior, equipment maintenance, and how to tie rescue-line knots.

His father worked for CalFire, and Chris was amazed at how much he had learned from him. When the class discussion turned to the life-threatening subject of pre-ignition and the use of the fire shelter, Chris already knew the lessons by heart. "Pre-ignition is what kills firefighters," his father had told him. "You'll be cutting line on the side of a mountain and there'll be a fire burning somewhere below you. That's when it happens." His father had lifted his hands upward. "Heat rises and it sucks the moisture out of the brush and trees and causes what's called pre-ignition. You have to watch for it. Sometimes a whole hillside will pre-heat and then all of a sudden, *bam*! It blows up in flames and God help you if you get caught in it. That's how firefighters get trapped and die. And if you ever have to use your 'shake and bake,'" his father had continued, referring to the fire shelter—an aluminum and woven fiberglass safety blanket of last resort, "you'll have less than sixty seconds to deploy it and get underneath. You can't practice that often enough."

Chris sat in the dark cabin of the Firehawk, the rumble of the big engines resonating through his body, and watched the eerie orange light in the sky. He leaned forward to get a better view—the glow was getting brighter, but he still couldn't make out the island or the water around it. "Hey Dad, I'm on the way to my first wildfire," he whispered to himself. His dad would be there by his side, advising him, and shepherding him through every step of the firefight.

"When you work one of those big wildland fires," his father had said, "you may spend two or three days at a time in a forest or on a mountainside. You'll be busting your ass cutting a fire line, you won't get much sleep, and you'll be eating crappy food. The heat will be incredible and the sweat will dry on your face in seconds. If you don't drink enough water, you'll dehydrate before you're even thirsty. You'll be sucking smoke and blowing black snot until you work yourself to exhaustion." He paused to make sure his son was paying attention, and then said, "and you'll love every minute of it."

When Chris finished his training, he had qualified for a helitack—helicopter attack—fire crew at Camp 8. Heading out to his first fire, he knew his father would be proud when he told him about it. He had once heard a story about a father and son, both wildland firefighters working for different departments, who had been surprised to meet each other working the same fire line. Chris had always imagined that someday he and his father would meet up in the same way. CalFire and L.A. County Fire? They worked together all the time. It could happen, and it would be the proudest day of Chris' life if he and his father were fighting a fire together.

The voice of his crew chief coming through the headset interrupted his thoughts. "The head of this fire is moving directly toward the Catalina Airport. We're going to drop down on the northwest side. We have a small window of time to cut line and create a defensible space around the main tower building and the aircraft hangar. Crews from Camps 2 and 9 are in the air and will join us shortly. Some of you are facing your first big fire, so pay attention to what's going on around you, listen to your crew leader, and don't lose your situational awareness."

The man sitting next to Chris nudged him in the ribs.

Chris lifted his headset away from his ear. "What?"

"They suspect it's an arson fire," the man said. "I heard a request for the Arson Unit."

"I hate to hear that," Chris responded. "My father died in an arson fire."

Once he knew the Firehawks were in the air, Brad left the ridge and made the slow drive to the Catalina Airport to meet the incoming camp crews. By the time he arrived, the first helicopter had landed and the men from Crew 1 were unloading their equipment. "I need you down there," Brad said, pointing to the points of light coming from the headlamps of the small group of volunteers at the far end of the runway.

While the camp crew moved into position, Brad huddled with the Camp 8 Superintendent and two crew leaders under a spotlight mounted on the back of the brushfire rig. "We're not going to stop this fire tonight," Brad said. "If we're lucky, we have three hours before it gets here and the best we can hope to do is deflect the flames and save the airport." He bent down and began to draw in the dirt with his finger. "There's shallow canyons out there full of brush and trees, and they will burn. We're here, at the north end of the airport and this is where the fire will hit us. We'll use the access road as part of the firebreak and begin cutting our fire line from there." He drew more lines in the dirt. "All we have to do is protect this end of the airport. There's a cliff at the other end, and not much fuel on the east side, so that's not a problem, and if we can push the fire out along the western flank, we'll just let it burn past us. That's all we can accomplish until the strike teams arrive in the morning and the air tankers are flying. We're going to try to contain it at Middle Ranch. Battalion Chief Turner will be incident commander and he's setting up his command post at the Catalina Freight ramp in Avalon." He looked at their expectant faces in the glare of the spotlight. "Questions?"

"Radio frequencies?" the Superintendent asked.

"Camp crews on tactical Blue-14. Strike teams will be on Blue-6 in the morning."

Ten minutes later, the second Firehawk arrived and the crews of wildland firefighters joined the volunteers at the end of the airport. Working with only the light from their headlamps, they cleared small trees and bushes with power saws, hacked away at patches of grass and undergrowth with shovels and the axe-like Pulaskis, and began to cut out a three-foot-wide fire line down to the hard soil. While they worked, the eerie glow of the approaching fire became bigger and brighter.

A call on her landline awakened Gina from a deep sleep. She raised her head from the table, feeling groggy and disoriented. She had dozed off in her kitchen. The telephone went silent for a moment and then rang again. She went to the counter and grabbed the receiver.

"This is Avalon Sheriff's Dispatch," a voice said. "We're notifying everyone at Middle Ranch. There's an immediate voluntary evacuation in effect. If you plan to leave, please do so in the next thirty minutes. The fire department will be on scene any moment for structure protection. If you plan to shelter in place—"

"Okay, thank you," Gina said. "I can't evacuate, I've got animals here and I've got to watch them." She hung up, turned on the coffee maker, and saw that was already 7:40 a.m. Why was it so dark? Out her kitchen window, it might have been dusk. The morning sun barely penetrated the thick blanket of brown smoke drifting across Middle Ranch, and tiny bits of ash were falling like a black snowfall. She hadn't lied, she did have animals to look after, but only two—the beaded lizard and the injured fox. Neither would survive outside in the smoke; they would have to come inside, into her lab. When she went into the living room to ask the boy to help, he was gone; only the imprint of his body, remained on the cushions. "Oh, no," Gina murmured, seeing visions of him fleeing the smoke and fire, running barefoot across the rugged landscape.

When she went outside to check on the lizard, she found him crouched down next to the cage. He was uttering the chirping sound and communing with the reptile.

"Hey," Gina shouted, as she approached the pen.

The boy looked up when he heard her. "Chik, chik, chik,"

"Oh, for Christ sake," she exploded, "Stop it, you're not a gecko. Stop the sounds and tell me your name. *Cómo te llamas?*"

He didn't respond.

"*Cómo te llamas?*" Gina insisted. He moved his lips but made no sound. "What?" Gina said. I can't hear you. Speak up!" She leaned in close to him.

"Jorge," he whispered, and then said it a little louder. "Jorge."

"Well, Jorge, help me drag your friend into my lab. There's a fire coming—and you probably started it."

At 7:50 a.m., the first of the Catalina Freight Line barges bumped up against the dock in Avalon and a red army of Los Angeles County Fire Department engines, water tankers, and support vehicles rumbled ashore. Chief Turner had already arrived by helicopter and assumed command. Fanned by a steady wind, the Paradise Fire had cut a five-mile swath down the center of Catalina in the ten hours since it began. It had burned south through heavy brush during its run, incinerated two campgrounds, sideswiped the Catalina Airport, and was now approaching the compound at Middle Ranch. The chief's top priority was to defend the Conservancy headquarters, and he immediately sent twenty engines and 100 firefighters for structure protection. The defense of the airport had been a success and the hand crews, reinforced by additional arrivals, had been moved south to join the battle at Middle Ranch.

Surrounded by his support staff and assisted by Brad, the chief unrolled a large topographical fire map and began to lay out a strategy to contain the fire. "We're gonna squeeze this sucker from its flanks, and force it to burn toward this empty reservoir," he said, stabbing the map with his pen. "We'll use Sweet Water Road as a firebreak on this side—I want hand crews deployed to cut a line and start back fires on the west flank. The Super Scoopers are on call, and we'll use them to drop water wherever we need it. The Firehawks can assist the strike teams at Middle Ranch. They can draw water from the holding tank at Helispot 55A." He bent over to take a closer look at the map. "Brad, what's this? Eagle's Nest Lodge?"

"The Conservancy was supposed to have sent a ranger over there late last night," Brad said. "It's in a remote spot."

"Well get a couple of crews over there," the chief said. "Try to find out from the Sheriff's Department if everyone has been evacuated."

Everything seemed to move at high speed as the defense of the Conservancy compound unfolded in Gina's front yard. She stood outside and watched engines and water tankers rolling in. Firefighters in yellow Nomex were everywhere, positioning their equipment around the Conservancy buildings. Men unrolled thick canvas fire hoses and connected them to the engines. Brown smoke gusted around her and then dispersed when two helicopters landed in the open field bordering her house and disgorged camp crews, weary after a busy night at the airport. Someone yelled, "… get a backfire started." Someone else shouted, "We need a water tender over here." A third firefighter warned, "Look for propane tanks." In the midst of the pandemonium, the first sign of the fire appeared over the hills to the north and Gina watched as it grew into a solid wall of flame and black smoke, moving toward the Middle Ranch compound. She stared at the blaze as if hypnotized until a firefighter ran up to her and said, "Ma'am, you should go inside. And keep your doors and windows closed."

Gina retreated to the house and watched from the kitchen window. The smoke got thicker, the fire came closer, and she was certain that all of Middle Ranch was about to be consumed by the hot, furious flames. More men than she could count were engaged in the battle, fighting every orange incursion with heavy blasts from their hoses. At one point, Gina heard water crashing down on the roof of her house and wondered if it was about to burst into flames. Across the field, she watched a helicopter come in low over the rangers' bunkhouse and release a cascade of water on an advancing finger of flames. In the midst of the crisis, she wondered what kind of damage thousands of gallons of saltwater was doing to the ecology of the island.

Late in the morning, a sudden calm prevailed. The frantic activity outside slowed, the smoke began to clear, and the flames were no longer visible. From her kitchen window, Gina saw that the fire had swept past and went to her front door to see the destruction. "Is it over?" she asked a nearby firefighter. "Did any of the buildings burn?"

"Just a barn and a storage shed at the east end of the compound," he told her. "Embers set their roofs on fire, but none of the other Conservancy structures were damaged."

Gina walked to the edge of the adjacent field and looked out beyond the defensive perimeter of the compound. The landscape resembled a charcoal drawing. Skeletons of trees smoldered, small patches of thick brush still burned, and the ground everywhere was scorched and blackened. The army of firefighters and engines that had mounted the defense was moving on, but men from the hand crews remained, scouring the surrounding terrain for hot spots.

In the late afternoon, Gina received a call from the Conservancy. The operator reported that the Paradise Fire had been declared partially contained after it hit the Thompson Reservoir two miles south of Middle Ranch. During the drought, the depth of rainwater in the basin had dropped to only a few feet, down from a level of over 1,200 acre-feet years earlier, but it was still enough to stop the advance of the fire. "The fire department said total containment will take another thirty-six hours, but it looks like the crisis is over. Spot fires are still burning and they say mopping up will last two to three days." The woman at the switchboard told Gina, "The real purpose of my call is to alert you that a meeting of Conservancy personnel is tentatively scheduled for tomorrow morning to begin to assess the damage caused by the fire. Check your e-mail tonight for details."

Just as Gina hung up, she heard someone banging on her front door. She assumed it was a Sheriff's deputy stopping by to make sure she was safe, but was surprised to find Brad and another firefighter standing on her porch. They both wore yellow brushfire gear streaked with soot, and looked very tired. The second man, much older than Brad, had a bushy, gray mustache.

"Afternoon, Gina," Brad said, his voice flat with exhaustion.

"Hello, Brad."

"This is Captain Will Larson. He's an arson investigator." Brad turned to the captain and said, "Will, this is Gina Winters."

"Ma'am," Will said.

Gina nodded. She already knew it was about the boy.

"Can we come in, please?" Will said. "I need to speak with you."

Gina moved aside and the two men stepped into her small living room.

Will opened his brush jacket and showed Gina the badge hanging from his shirt pocket. "Ma'am," he said, "my team has been out to examine the spot above Paradise Cove, the area where the fire started. We're certain that the fire was incendiary, that is, it was set intentionally. We spent the better part of the day looking at the canyon and ridge area. We've got more work to do, but based on the burn pattern, we believe that the point of origin was just below the top of the ridge, on the ocean side. We found a distinct trail coming from the beach up through the brush. It looks like someone, possibly the arsonist, dragged something up from down below. Whoever it was, was wearing sandals and lost them during the climb. I have them in my truck. They're small, and I would say worn by a teen-ager. Brad, Captain Stillman, told me that—"

"I told him that you were up on the ridge last night," Brad interrupted. "When you drove past me on the way back, I thought you had someone with you in your pickup."

"I did," Gina said. "I found a young boy hiding in the brush and brought him back here." She saw Brad and the arson investigator exchange glances.

"Is he still here?" Will asked.

"He's in my lab, looking at the salamanders."

"How old is he?" Will asked.

"I'm not sure," Gina said.

"Did he say how old he is?" Brad asked.

"He's young," Gina said. "He could be eleven or twelve. I asked him, and he said he doesn't know."

"How is that possible?" Brad sounded impatient.

"He's not quite normal and he doesn't talk much, just says a few words in Spanish. He did tell me he's from Mexico."

"What were you planning on doing with him?" Brad asked. "He probably started this fire."

Gina heard his hostile tone. "I was going to call the Sheriff's Department, but there's been a fire emergency, in case you hadn't noticed."

Will smiled and asked, "What did he drag up from the beach?"

"What did he drag?" Gina asked.

"Something left a trail up through the vegetation," Will said. "Was he pulling a sled or something?"

"A sled?" Gina said. "What kind of a sled? When I found him, it was dark and I couldn't see much, but he didn't seem to have anything with him." She studied Will's face to determine whether he believed her, and decided she had to get rid of the lizard as soon as possible, before anyone discovered it.

"Can I talk to the boy?" Will said. "I want to ask him some questions."

"Do you speak Spanish?" Gina asked.

"No, ma'am" Will said.

"Then I'll have to translate for you," Gina said. "And don't expect too much. If he does answer, it's likely to be a word or two. I'm not sure what's wrong with him, but he's very shy, and the less people standing around him, the better. Brad, unless you have to be present, I suggest you go outside." Gina felt very uncomfortable with Brad in her living room.

"Can I wait in the kitchen?" Brad said. "I'm so tired I'm about to collapse. I'd like to splash some water on my face and have something to drink."

"Help yourself, I'll get the boy," Gina said, and went out to find Jorge. She found him just where she had left him, in her lab, with his face pressed against the glass, watching the brown and gray arboreal salamanders clinging to the small logs and stones in the vivarium. "There's a man here," Gina said to him. "He wants to ask you some questions about the fire and what you were doing yesterday."

Including this visit, Brad had been in Gina's kitchen four times during their affair. He stood at the sink, ran the cold water, and splashed it on his face, then leaned down and drank from the tap. He had been awake now for more than twenty-four hours, surveying the fire on Paradise Cove ridge, supervising the defense of the north end of the airport, and then assisting his battalion chief at the incident command center. He felt bone tired, had a headache, and was in a rotten mood. He looked around Gina's messy kitchen through bleary eyes. A faint cooking aroma, possibly the smell of breakfast bacon, hung in the air. The counter was strewn with containers and feeding dishes that Gina used in her lab and in the animal pens. Her boots and a pair of work gloves lay on the old wood-plank floor. The tiny kitchen table was just as he remembered it, but a small, forlorn potted cactus was new. Standing at the sink, Brad thought of first time Gina had prepared dinner for him while he listened to Will Larson begin to question the boy and

"Son, did you set that fire?"

Brad's soon to be ex-wife was a gourmet cook, but Gina had barely mastered the basics. The dinner had been nothing special, just pasta with meatballs and a salad, but Brad had been captivated by the gesture. Gina had opened a bottle of wine, lit a candle, and turned off the kitchen lights.

"Why did you do it?"

Brad remembered how completely spellbound he had felt. When they sat down, he'd looked at her in the flickering candlelight and said, "You look so beautiful. Thanks for inviting me for dinner."

"You're welcome," she responded. "After dinner you can show your appreciation."

A wave of lust had washed over him. "How about right now?" He almost tipped over the table when he pulled her up.

"The pasta will get ruined," she laughed, letting him tug her into the second bedroom.

"Let it," he said, and fell down on top of her.

"How did you start the fire? Did you use matches?"

Looking back, Brad recognized that evening in Gina's house as the turning point in the disintegration of his marriage. At the time, he felt he might be falling in love with her and knew that he was in trouble. Now, standing by the sink while Will questioned the Mexican boy in the other room, Brad understood how one-sided their affair had actually been. He tried to count the number of times he had been with Gina. A hundred? More? While he was making love to her, she was just screwing him. Had she ever loved him? He had waited, and hoped it would happen, but now in hindsight, he understood how naive he had been. What a fool he was. Gina would never have fallen in love with him. He wasn't sure if she had ever really cared about him. She had just wanted sex. Wasn't that the man's role in an affair? Brad decided if he were patient, there might come a time when he could repay the favor to Gina. What goes around, comes around. He walked back into the living room and stared at her. In the absence of any sexual desire, she looked like an ordinary woman—a woman he hated.

As soon as Brad and the arson investigator departed, Gina began searching for Richard's number at the Reptile Institute. Now that the boy had been questioned, it was just a matter of time before someone found out about the lizard. When she called Richard, she got an answering machine. After all the years, his voice sounded the same and she left a message: "Hi Richard, this is Gina Winters. I hope you're well. We haven't spoken in a long time, but please call me—I'm still at the Conservancy. It's important, I have a Motagua Valley beaded lizard in my animal lab and I wonder if you could find a home for it."

Gina had barely hung up when her phone rang.

"You have a Motagua Valley beaded lizard?"

"Hello, Richard," Gina said. "How have you been?"

"Do you really have a Motagua?"

"Yes."

"You're certain? It's not a Gila Monster, is it?"

"Christ, Richard, I'm not stupid," Gina hissed. "It's not a Gila Monster and it's not a Mexican beaded. It's a Motagua Valley beaded lizard. I recognized it the minute I saw it."

"Sorry, I uh… where'd you get it?"

"You're not going to believe this, but, well, we had a fire here on the island—actually it's still burning—and I went out to check on a bald eagle nest, and I found a kid, a Mexican kid, hiding in the brush. He had a cage he was dragging around. The lizard was in it."

"A kid and a cage? C'mon Gina, you expect me to believe that? What's the real story?"

"It's true Richard, and I don't know what to do with it. I can't keep it. I thought you might have an idea."

"Is it healthy?"

"It appears to be."

"Can you send me a couple of photos?"

"Sure, I'll do it as soon as we hang up."

"The only thing to do with it is return it to Guatemala. I'm flying down there next week. Maybe I could take it with me."

"You're going to Guatemala?"

"Yeah, I'm going to collect specimens for the Los Angeles County Natural History Museum. They're building a huge rainforest exhibit with a reptile garden, and I've been hired to stock it. Want to hear something spooky?"

"What?"

"I'm also speaking about endangered reptiles at an environmental conference in Guatemala City. I was in touch with an agricultural engineer down there, a man named Alejandro Luna, who found someone to help me collect the specimens. He was supposed to speak at the conference as well, but it turns out he was killed three weeks ago in a cartel gun battle in Culiacán. Can you believe that?"

"You couldn't get me to Mexico. I'm happy to stay here on Catalina, even with the wildfires. Too much violence down there."

"Let me mull it over and I'll call you back. The Museum has chartered a plane, so it would be easy to take the lizard with me back to Guatemala."

"That would be fantastic. Thanks, Richard, nice to talk to you."

"Don't bullshit me Gina. You need something, that's the only reason you're calling."

On the morning after he questioned the young Mexican boy, Will Larson sat with Brad and Chief Turner from Battalion 17 in the shade of a crew truck parked at the incident command post. Will was one of the best in the Arson Investigation Unit. He'd been at it for fifteen years and had been all over Los Angeles County investigating suspicious building fires, automobiles torched for insurance, and blazes started by vandals in vacant lots. What he enjoyed the most, however, and what he was the best at doing, was working wildland fires. Will had worked all the big arson incidents in the county, including the Station Fire that had consumed 160,000 acres in the Angeles National Forest and resulted in the death of two firefighters. He had probed accidental wildland fires started by lightning strikes and sparks from road equipment; he had investigated burns set by careless campers in places where open flames were not allowed; and he had worked the true arson situations that were intentionally started by psychopaths. Will had seen it all, and he accepted the fact that arson investigation was as much an art as a science. Solving any arson fire required both painstaking work and good luck. He had spent weeks trying to pinpoint the origin of a fire, walking through burnt stands of trees, looking at the "gatoring" on the wood—the pucker on the side of the tree where the flames hit it. He had spent countless hours on his hands and knees, studying the ground through magnification glasses, seeking the remnants of burnt matches or other clues to how a fire had been started. He had interviewed arson suspects, listened to their lies, and come back to interview them again. It was a tough business. Arson fires could take months or even years to investigate, and nine out of ten went unsolved. Sometimes a random bit of information or a chance event proved to be the key to the solution. The Paradise Fire had been an outlier, a slam-dunk—it had taken less than twenty-four hours. Brad had simply led him to the arsonist. "You look a helluva lot better today than you did yesterday," he said to Brad.

"I've only had about two hours' sleep in a day and a half," Brad said. He yawned and stretched his arms. "I'm getting too old for that kind of stuff."

"So what have we got?" Chief Turner asked Will.

"This one was easy," Will told the battalion chief. "My crew scoured the canyon up toward the top of the ridge and it took less than six hours to identify the point of origin. We could spend some more time and study the burn patterns, but I don't see any purpose. We've determined that the Mexican boy started the fire, and that's all that matters."

"And there's no doubt?" the chief asked.

"I spoke to the Conservancy woman, what's her name..." Will paused to look at his notes. "Gina Winters. She said she found the boy in the brush, maybe twenty yards from where we suspect the fire started. When I talked to him, I didn't get a hell of a lot of information, but he did admit starting it." Will paused, drank from his water bottle, and smoothed his mustache with the back of his hand. "There are a few loose ends. I understand enough Spanish to know that she wasn't translating his answers word for word, and that some of what the kid said didn't make sense."

"Like what?" Brad asked.

"Well," Will said, "he admitted he started the fire because he was cold, then he said the lizard told him to do it."

"The lizard?" Chief Turner said. "What lizard?"

"I have no idea," Will said. "Then there's the trail up through the brush. I'm convinced the kid dragged something up there before he started the fire. I'd like to know what it was."

"Maybe he had a pet dragon," Brad said. "Breathing fire."

"I dunno," Will said. "There are unanswered questions, but the basic facts are cut and dried. We know the kid started the fire. Our arsonist is a J.O."

"A J.O?" Chief Turner said. "What's a J.O?"

"A juvenile offender," Will said. "In fact, he may not even be old enough to be a J.O. You have to be at least thirteen. The Winters woman thinks he may be younger than that."

"He's an illegal and he has no documentation," Brad told the chief. "There's no way to determine how old he is."

"I don't like where this is headed," the Chief Turner said, and frowned. "This kid set fire to six thousand acres and did a lot of destruction. By the time we're finished here, it's going to cost the county a couple of million dollars just to fight the fire. Not to mention how much damage it did to the wildlife and the island itself. Those Conservancy people are fanatics about the environment. They're still recovering from the last damn fire. Don't tell me this kid is just going to walk away from this."

"Can you hold a twelve-year-old boy accountable?" Will shrugged his shoulders. "I'm not the D.A., and he's the one who makes the decisions, but if you ask me, there's no way he'll prosecute. The kid's too young and he's not a repeat offender. Besides, there's no intent. He said he was just trying to stay warm, and I buy that. He can't make any restitution and in fact, he's not even old enough to send to a juvenile counseling program. This will turn out to be just a case of 'lecture and release.'"

"Gina Winters?" the chief asked Brad. "Isn't that the woman you're… um… seeing?"

"Past tense," Brad said. "Not anymore." He glanced at Chief Turner. "And it was supposed to be a secret."

"What was she doing out there last night?" the chief asked.

Brad was amazed. How did his battalion chief find out about Gina? Who else knew? Did Ann? Was that what had fueled her anger and finished their marriage?

"Brad," the chief repeated. "Hello? Do you know what Gina Winters was doing out there last night?"

"She went up to the ridge to check on a bald eagle's nest," Brad said. "She said she found the kid and took him home."

"So there you have it," Will said. "Our arsonist is an underage kid, an illegal. The D.A. will probably turn him over to ICE and let them deal with him. And they'll probably deport him, send him back to wherever he came from."

"The island residents will be furious," Brad said. "The last guy who started a fire here is still in prison."

"Well, at least we can take credit for a successful investigation," the chief said. "We can announce that after some extraordinary hard work by our tireless investigators," he winked at Will and went on, "we identified the arsonist—an underage illegal who's been turned over to the proper authorities. That work for you Brad?"

Brad shrugged his shoulders. "It's all we've got."

"Then we're done," Will said. "I'll talk to the D.A. and notify the Sheriff about the boy. He stood up and smoothed his mustache again. "Remember that big wildland fire in Ventura County a few years ago? The Oaks Fire? I was on the investigation. Turned out it was started by Mexican gang members. Now that was arson with a motive. They had beaten someone to death and were trying to get rid of the body."

Ryan hadn't had time to call Sharon to tell her that as soon as he had some time off, they would be going away for few days. He and Victor had been working non-stop since the cellphone was taken off the body of Felix Cabrera. A tech from the Digital Evidence Lab had downloaded the call history and contacts. Forty-nine numbers were extracted, half of which started with 52, the Mexican country code, and a dozen of those were in the 667 Culiacán /Sinaloa area code. A team of analysts were already trying to link the U.S. numbers to known cartel members so Ryan could establish probable cause and obtain Federal wiretap warrants. The international numbers had been passed on to the Mexican police through the DEA's office in Mexico City.

Ryan remained convinced that what he and Victor had observed off Catalina was an aborted drug deal. Felix Cabrera's presence in the nearby waters made him even more certain. He had reviewed the skimpy file the Bird's Eye task force had put together on the *Exchange Rate* and its registered owner Pella Delgado, but didn't learn much. When Ryan accessed the DEA's own file on Delgado, it was just as incomplete. Beyond the fact that Delgado lived in Culiacán, the intel was a collection of rumors and hearsay. One informant was quoted as saying, "This guy is a rattlesnake. He's powerful, deadly, and you'll never grab hold of him."

The dossier did include a single picture of Delgado, a grainy newspaper photo taken in Mexico City, showing him coming out of a restaurant with a woman named Susana Manterola. Ryan ran a magnifying glass over the picture, studied Delgado, and then moved on to the woman. "Wow, Victor," he said. "You have to see the woman he's with. She's gorgeous. She must be an actress or a movie star."

Victor took the magnifier and focused on Delgado. "Is this all we've got? No satellite images? It's hard to tell what he looks like. I couldn't recognize him if he were sitting here."

There were references in the file to Delgado's possible role as banker to the Sinaloa Cartel, but nothing concrete, no real documentation. If he really was who he was rumored to be, the man had maintained an incredibly low profile. When Ryan read that Delgado's nickname was rumored to be *El Dedo de Oro*, he asked Victor, "What does it mean? Golden Dick?"

"Goldfinger, you idiot," Victor said.

"Goldfinger?" Ryan laughed. "Could the Sinaloa Cartel's top banker really be called Goldfinger? That has to be a joke, right? If we raid his house, are we gonna find gold bars stashed in his closet?"

"*We* won't be doing any raiding," Victor said. "That's strictly for the Mexican Federal Police, or the marines."

"Well, maybe if we can document a strong enough case against him, they'll let us tag along. We just have to find more information on Golden Dick," he said to Victor.

In the frenzy of events, they had forgotten about the boy on the dock until a call came from the Catalina station of the Los Angeles County Sheriff's Department. "That kid you're looking for," a sergeant told Ryan, "the one who was left on the dock at Paradise Cove? We've located him—it looks like he's responsible for starting the fire over here. Right now, he's at the Catalina Conservancy compound. We're taking an ICE agent over to see him in the morning. If you want to come, I can get you on the bird."

"Bingo," Ryan said to Victor. "Maybe this kid can fill in some of the blanks on Golden Dick."

Gina heard the helicopter overhead and assumed it was one of the Firehawks that had been shuttling back and forth all day. The sound stopped moving and got louder, and when she went outside, she saw the underside of a gold and green Sheriff's Department helicopter dropping down in the open field beside her house. As it settled, the rotors kicked up a windstorm of ash and soot, and Gina turned away and covered her face until the engine stopped. She half-expected the arson investigator, coming back to arrest the boy, but when she turned she saw two men and a woman climbing out of the helicopter. She recognized Sergeant Barnes—or maybe it was Barney—a bear of a man who was finishing out his years with the Sheriff's Department at the Avalon station. The second person off the helicopter was a much younger man who wore sunglasses, jeans, and a dark polo shirt. As soon as Gina saw his pistol and the badge swinging on a chain around his neck, she knew he was a federal agent. The third person was a tall woman wearing dark green pants and a matching shirt. Her badge was on her belt, and she didn't have a gun. Had Fish and Game already come to arrest her for possession of the Motagua Lizard?

"Morning, Ms. Winter," the sergeant said.

Gina, nodding, remembered his last name was Brady.

He gestured at the woman. "This is Immigration and Customs Enforcement Agent Sher—"

"Shcherbyna," the ICE agent said.

Gina gave the woman a quick once-over and didn't like her. She was slim, with high cheekbones, and wore her blond hair in a short ponytail that hung out of the back of her ICE ball cap. Gina couldn't see her eyes behind the aviator sunglasses, but guessed they were blue. Gina had never met an attractive woman she liked. It had been that way since she was a child—she regarded every decent-looking woman as a sexual competitor.

The second man stepped forward and extended his hand. "I'm Special Agent Ryan Daniels, DEA."

"DEA?" He was an interesting-looking guy. Gina shook his hand. "You here to bust me because of my meth lab?" She gave him a quick, flirtatious smile and wondered why these people had to arrive when she was wearing baggy cargo pants and a dirty work shirt.

"The DEA has been looking for a young boy, possibly a Mexican national," the sergeant said. "The fire department notified us that—"

"He came off a boat," Ryan interrupted. "Three days ago. Actually, it was a yacht, and it may have been transporting drugs. Is he here with you?"

"Yes," Gina said. "I found him the night I went out to check on the fire."

"I have to interview him and determine his status," the ICE agent said.

"And I've got some questions to ask him," the DEA agent said.

"An arson investigator was here yesterday," Gina said, "and scared the kid to death. If you plan on getting any answers from him, go easy. He doesn't speak English and he doesn't say much even in Spanish."

"I'm heading over to Avalon on the copter," the sergeant said. "We'll be back in less than an hour." "Come in," Gina said to the other two, and watched the DEA man check out the ICE agent's bubble butt as they entered her house.

"The boy's name is Jorge," Gina said. "Do either of you speak Spanish?"

"I do," the ICE agent said.

She spoke Spanish? Now Gina truly hated the blond with the impossible last name. "He's out back with his lizard," she said.

When the two agents returned to the house, Jorge trailed after them. Gina saw him cowering by the door, one foot inside the living room. "Well?" she asked.

"You're right, he's not a big talker," the ICE agent said, ignoring Jorge's presence.

"What's that strange noise he makes?" the DEA agent asked. "He answered half the questions with little chirps."

"That's the sound of a gecko," Gina said.

"He is frightened," the ICE agent said. "He asked me if he was going to jail."

"He says he wants to go home. To Culiacán," the DEA agent said. "You know that's a drug hot spot. That's where the Sinaloa Cartel is based."

"The problem is," the ICE agent said, "there may not be anyone to send him back to. He says his mother is dead and he never knew his father."

"So where has he been living?" Gina asked.

"I'm not sure," the ICE agent said. "First he said he lived on the street. Then he said he lived with different people. Finally he said he was living in a fancy house with money."

"An expensive house?" Gina asked.

"To be exact, *una mansión elegante con mucha lana en el sótano*. A mansion with money in the basement, whatever that means," the ICE agent said.

"It means," the DEA agent interrupted, "that he was living with a cartel boss. He's probably talking about a hoard of drug money." He glanced at Jorge. "This boy could have information that's important to our case. I'll have to come back with my partner and an interpreter and spend some time with him. We're going to have a lot of questions." He turned to the ICE agent. "Are you going to detain him?"

"I have to discuss his status with my supervisor. He's an unaccompanied minor and I'm not sure what the procedure is. We could take him into custody, but we're not really set up to handle someone this young when he's by himself." She looked at Gina. "He might qualify for what we call SIJS—Special Immigration Juvenile Status—and then he could actually stay in the U.S. But to do that, someone would have to step forward as his guardian. Would that be you?"

"Me?" Gina said. "No, I'm not taking responsibility for him. The kid just set fire to Catalina Island."

"Could he stay with you—just temporarily?" the DEA agent asked Gina. "It would be better if he were here instead of in detention or foster care. When we talk to him, we want him somewhere he's relaxed and not frightened."

Gina wasn't anxious to have the boy around any longer than necessary, but at least it would ensure the return of the young DEA agent. The next time, with a little notice, she would wear something decent. "I guess I could take care of him for a few more days," she said.

Flying back to Los Angeles on the Sheriff's helicopter, Ryan tried to hide his excitement. The case he and Victor were working was looking even bigger and more important than he had first imagined. *El Dedo de Oro.* A kingpin's stronghold in Culiacán. A basement full of money. They were going all the way to the top of the Sinaloa Cartel! At some point, the DEA would share this information with the Mexican authorities and convince them to start a parallel investigation. Ryan imagined a new, jacked-up version of his favorite fantasy—this time he was wearing his Kevlar DEA vest and joining the Mexican Federal Police in a massive takedown in Culiacán. After shooting his way into Delgado's house, Ryan would be the first one into the basement, where he would discover a cache of millions of dollars hidden in a storeroom.

As soon as he got back to his office, Ryan planned to put together an album of pictures of the men suspected to be at the top of the Sinaloa Cartel. Maybe the boy would recognize some of them as visitors to Delgado's house. He hoped the kid could pinpoint where he'd been living. Getting a satellite image of the area would take weeks, but maybe they could show him a printout of a Google map. Ryan needed details about the house, especially a description of the basement full of money. Finally, he wanted intel on Delgado—what his habits were, what he did during the day, whether he had a girlfriend. Ryan needed a lot of information, and the more he imagined the boy living with a top cartel boss, the more questions he had. The boy was young and shy and Ryan wasn't sure how much information they would actually come away with, but he intended to do his best. He and Victor had a lot to do to prepare for the interview.

As the helicopter settled onto the landing pad on top of the Roybal Building, Ryan looked at the ICE agent sitting across from him. She was much more attractive than Sharon.

She removed her sunglasses, returned his gaze with cornflower blue eyes, and smiled.

"Do you carry a weapon?" he asked.

"Not when I'm interviewing a twelve-year-old."

"Otherwise?"

"A Glock 43."

"Same here." He tapped the pistol in his hip holster. "Can I have your phone number?"

"Sure." She raked his face again with her beautiful blue eyes, reached into her pocket and pulled out her card. "Call me."

They were both law enforcement. Ryan thought they would have a lot in common.

VIII | THE LIZARD

The Motagua Valley beaded lizard follows his instincts and continues the only existence he knows. He moves through the river valley, picking up familiar scents, seeking food, looking for a mate, and searching for a burrow. He has few natural enemies, but faces extinction due to habitat destruction, illegal collection, and fearful, superstitious local people who believe the myths about him.

The lizard's territory in the Motagua Valley, is a tropical dry forest, one of the most endangered ecosystems on earth. Only 35,000 acres remain—about the size of Disney World—it has been seriously degraded. The floor of the valley is being irrigated to grow tobacco, cantaloupe, and other crops, while the hillsides are being stripped of their original vegetation and planted with corn. It is estimated that more than half of the lizard's original home range has already disappeared.

In the Guatemalan habitat, there are estimated to be less than 400 Motagua Valley beaded lizards remaining. Zoo Atlanta has a conservation program based in Guatemala dedicated to researching and protecting the Motagua Valley beaded lizard; it has purchased 1,000 acres of prime beaded lizard habitat and has begun construction of a breeding facility. Zoo Atlanta and the San Diego Zoo have managed to hatch less than a dozen Motagua Valley beaded lizards in captivity.

The Motagua Valley beaded lizard is protected as an endangered species under Appendix II of the *Convention on International Trade in Endangered Species*, and is listed as a threatened species on the Guatemalan "Red List."

The Lacey Act makes it a federal crime to import or sell protected wildlife, but U.S. Customs officials continue to encounter numerous smuggling violations, as exemplified by the two well-known reptile dealers who were recently caught with beaded lizards in the floor panels of their small aircraft.

The Center for Biological Diversity reports: *We're currently experiencing the worst spate of species die-offs since the loss of the dinosaurs 65 million years ago. Although extinction is a natural phenomenon, it occurs at a natural "background" rate of only about one to five species per year. Scientists estimate we're now losing species at 1,000 to 10,000 times the background rate, with literally dozens going extinct every day. It could be a scary future indeed, with as many as 30 to 50 percent of all species possibly heading toward extinction by mid-century.*

IX | JOSE MIGUEL

"This airport sucks. The runway starts at the edge of a 1500-foot cliff, and there's a strong downdraft on the approach. It's very tricky."

"Sounds like a carrier landing."

"Yeah, except carriers don't have animals on the flight deck. Here you have to watch out for stray bison on the runway."

"Bison? On Catalina Island? You've got to be kidding."

Richard Reed sat on a jump seat jammed into the cramped cockpit behind the two pilots of the DC3, and listened to their conversation through the headphones. He had once visited the working end of a Boeing 737, and had sat in the copilot's seat on a sleek King Air 350 several times, but he had never seen anything like the instrument panel and controls of the DC3. Everything looked old. When the Los Angeles County Museum of Natural History told him they would charter a plane to transport his equipment and supplies to Guatemala and to bring back the reptiles and samples of the flora, he didn't expect an aircraft that had made its debut in World War II.

"Is this plane uh…airworthy?" Richard asked.

"Not to worry," one of the pilots replied. "It's perfectly safe. The airframe has been retrofitted and it has new avionics and hydraulics.

Plus, we're flying the latest Pratt and Whitney turbines. This is a fantastic aircraft—it can land and takeoff anywhere. It's perfect for Guatemala."

"I'll take your word for it," Richard said, and looked down through a small cabin window. It looked like God had taken a blowtorch and burned a black swath of the island from north to south. The airport seemed to have been spared, but Richard could see where the fire had burned past it on one side and then spread out as it progressed toward the center of the island. The fire emergency was over now, and the airport had reopened, but patches of white smoke still drifted up from the charred ground. From the air, he saw scattered crews dressed in the orange uniforms of the fire camp inmates, working around smoldering trees and other hot spots.

The pitch of the engines changed and the aircraft dipped one wing as it circled above the airport, an oasis of green and brown amid the blackened landscape. As the DC3 began its approach, Richard watched as the cliff and the end of the landing strip appeared through the front windshield. He grasped the edge of his seat as the plane hit the pavement with a hard bump, bounced once, and then settled onto the runway. They rolled past a small building with a few cars parked around it, a two-story control tower, several small aircraft hangars, and finally a red Catalina Services bobtail fuel truck, before the pilot cut the engines. By the time the propellers stopped and Richard released his seatbelt, a black pickup had appeared beside the airplane. He watched as a woman stepped out of the driver's-side door and shaded her eyes from the sun. It was Gina.

Richard could care less about Gina, but he was eager to get a look at the Motagua Valley beaded lizard. Although he was a recognized authority on reptiles and had seen countless Gila Monsters and a few Mexican beaded lizards, he had never seen a live Motagua. How many people had? It was one of the rarest creatures on earth and wouldn't be found in a local petting zoo. Seeing one was very special and provided bragging rights—it would enhance his credentials.

It had been a busy year. He had begun by conferring with the museum curators and drawing up a proposed list of reptiles and plants for their new multi-million dollar exhibit. Once they'd agreed on the inventory, the agonizing process of obtaining permits started, and there were times when Richard wondered if it would ever end. Getting waivers and import authorizations from the U.S. Fish and Wildlife Service, U.S. Customs and Border Protection, and the Agriculture Department's Animal and Plant Health Inspection Service, as well as from the California Department of Fish and Game, had been bad enough. On the Guatemalan side, he had spent months coaxing export certificates from bureaucrats who seemed to only work one day a week. It had finally all come together. Gina had happened to call on the very day when he had completed assembling the collection of cages and traps, clothing, camping equipment, and other supplies that he planned to take with him. If she had tried to reach him a week later, he would have already been on the way to Guatemala.

Gina hadn't seen Richard in almost ten years, but she was still surprised when the cargo door opened and he came down the steps. He had lost most of his hair and gained weight. A spare tire of fat around his midsection pressed out against his khaki shirt and Gina wondered how she could have ever been attracted to him, even if only for a couple of weeks. Seeing him standing on the runway made her appreciate how handsome Brad was. Gina was feeling lonely. She had been thinking about Brad since he came to her house with the arson investigator and, as the days passed, she missed him and wanted to see him again. Brad was a good man and now she wasn't even certain why she had treated him so badly. She had called his cellphone and sent a couple of text messages, but he hadn't responded.

"Hello, Gina," Richard said. "It's been a while, hasn't it?"

"Yes, it has," she said. "Nice to see you."

Is it, Richard wondered. "Quite a fire you had here."

"I suppose it could have been much worse. They stopped it near the Conservancy headquarters at Middle Ranch. If it had gone on, the fire department said it might have burned all the way to Avalon. That would have really been a disaster. The whole town's built out of wood, and 3,000 people would have been in the water, swimming to Los Angeles."

"What about the wildlife?"

"Too early to tell—we haven't really had a chance to do a survey. The Island Foxes were just beginning to make a comeback. I suppose the only good news is that we burned off a lot of dead wood and brush that would have fed the next fire."

Richard glanced at the thin, dark boy who had emerged from the pickup and was now standing next to Gina. "Who's this?"

"This is Jorge, the boy I mentioned—the one I found with the lizard. He's very attached to it, so I brought him along to say goodbye." Gina looked at the DC3. "You headed directly to Guatemala?"

"We have to refuel in Mazatlan. It's a long trip, so I don't have much time. Where's the Motagua?"

"Here." Gina walked to the back of the pickup, lowered the tailgate, and pulled away the blanket covering the cage. "Thanks for coming to get it. I didn't know what to do with it."

As soon as the cage was uncovered, Richard watched the boy jump up onto the truck bed, bend over the lizard's cage, and utter a strange, chirping sound.

"What's that?" Richard said. "He almost sounds like a gecko."

"It *is* a gecko sound," Gina said, giving him a knowing look. "He thinks he's talking to the lizard."

Richard leaned over the side of the pickup to see the reptile. It was immobile, sitting on top of the wood chips and moss in the cage. The only sign that it was alive was the flicking of its forked tongue. "It's beautiful," he said. "Amazing." Richard bent closer to the cage and saw the distinct yellow and black bands on the creature's tail that differentiated it from its cousin, the Mexican beaded lizard. The lizard began to sway from side to side and hiss. "Do you know the legend about these creatures?"

"Legend?" Gina said.

"Yes. The folklore says that they bring bad luck, maybe even death, to people who capture them."

"No, I've never heard that, but I guess we're in line for some good luck."

"How do you figure that?"

"Because we're releasing it, sending it back to its home."

Richard chuckled and said, "Well, I hope you're right. A local guide is meeting us when we get there. I found him through the agricultural engineer I told you about, the one who was killed in Culiacán. The guide's supposed to help us find our specimens, but before we head out, I'm going to ask him to take the lizard back to its natural habitat."

"Culiacán—that's where this boy says he's from." Gina looked at Jorge. "The DEA told me he came to Catalina on a boat, possibly a Mexican drug boat, but that still doesn't explain what he was doing with this lizard."

A drug boat. Of course. Another piece of the puzzle fell into place. When the man—his name was Felix Cabrera— first contacted Richard and asked him to design a habitat inside his home for a Gila Monster, Richard had said he was too busy. The man persisted, kept calling back, and wouldn't take no for an answer. He had offered an extraordinary amount of money, $10,000, and mentioned that he could pay in cash. Richard had been wary, but the money had been too good to pass up. He had agreed to do the work, but said he would only take a check, not cash.

When Richard arrived at the house in Santa Ana to begin drawing up the specifications, Cabrera started asking questions. "There's another kind of venomous lizard. Right? One that comes from Guatemala?"

"Are you talking about a beaded lizard?" Richard said. "A Motagua Valley beaded lizard?"

"Yeah, that's it. It's just like a Gila Monster, right? So it could it live in the same space and eat the same food?"

"It could. Sure, if you had one." Richard had wondered what kind of person would build a habitat for a Gila Monster in the middle of his home. Then he understood. Cabrera, who said he owned a frozen-food trucking business, was probably a drug dealer. They had a thing for exotic animals, and that included reptiles. Richard was building a habitat to show off the man's next trophy, a Motagua beaded lizard, and not a common Gila Monster. He had decided the best thing to do was to keep his mouth shut, finish his work, collect his money, and never come back. The elaborate enclosure he designed had glass walls, a small water feature, and included places where the lizard—whatever it was—could burrow underground. Cabrera was thrilled with what Richard created, paid him with a check, and that had been the end of it. Richard had heard no more. When Gina called, he was still puzzling over how Cabrera, living in Orange County, California, could get his hands on a Guatemalan beaded lizard. Now he understood—the lizard had been sent up from Central America on a boat. Something must have gone wrong with the delivery plan and somehow this strange kid had ended up with it.

Richard started to lift the cage off the bed of the pickup. It was heavy. "Hey," he shouted to one of the pilots, "can you give me a hand with this?"

"You don't want your lizard friend to die, do you?" the *gringa* had asked Jorge the day before in her strange Spanish. "He can't stay in that cage. It's cruel. He is a rare creature, and has to return to his home in Guatemala, to the place he came from. Tomorrow he's going back."

What the *gringa* had said was true. The Lizard King shouldn't be kept in a cage, he should be free. After the *gringa* spoke to him, Jorge spent the rest of the day sitting next to the cage, telling the Lizard King goodbye. *I know you want to go home Lizard King, and the gringa says it will happen tomorrow. I will find a way to go home too. I have something I must do in Culiacán. I wish I could take you with me. I wish we could be together forever.* Jorge had reached inside the cage to touch the Lizard King once more. He felt the familiar warmth, the same electric sensation flooding through his body, and it comforted him. Jorge had barely slept, knowing that the Lizard King would be sent away in the morning. He had arisen before sunrise to spend the last precious hours with his friend. Now the moment of departure had arrived and Jorge stood on the cement airstrip, holding back his tears while he watched the men load the Lizard King onto the airplane. He loved the Lizard King and would never forget him.

The *gringa* was speaking English with the man who had arrived on the airplane, but Jorge heard words he understood—"Mazatlan" and "Culiacán."

Jorge hated *El Norte*. Nothing but bad things had happened since Dedo put him on the boat. First Maria Gabriela deserted him and then he had to fight the man on the dock who had tried to take away the Lizard King. When the *gringa* rescued him from the fire, he hoped he would be safe, but people had come and threatened him. First, the *bombero* said he could be punished for starting the fire. Then *La funcionario de inmigración* said he was an illegal and might be put in detention. And finally, the men from *La DEA*—they were the worst. They wanted information about *El Dedo*, his friends, and his home in Culiacán, and spent two whole days showing him pictures and maps and demanding answers to their questions. Jorge didn't care what happened to Dedo—if they arrested him and took away his money, it would be *la retribución*, payback for all the rotten things he had done. Jorge had told *La DEA* everything he knew, but they weren't satisfied. They would come back and demand more information, and if he had nothing left to tell them, he was afraid they would arrest him.

Jorge didn't want to end up in an American jail. He wanted to get away. Culiacán was his home. Even though he had no family waiting there for him, it was where all his memories—good and bad—resided. After all the years, he still thought of his *mamá* and missed her. And the man? The one with the tattoo of the skull and barbwire on the back of his neck? The one who murdered her? Jorge had not forgotten him either. Culiacán was where Jorge belonged—he had something important to do there. He had to find the man with the tattoo and kill him.

They had a lot of gear on board to take to Central America, but there was plenty of space inside the DC3 for the lizard. Once the cage had been secured, the new Pratt and Whitney turbines came to life, the propellers began to spin, and the aircraft turned and prepared for takeoff.

Gina had driven partway down the runway to force two wandering Bison aside with her pickup and Richard peered out through the windshield to see whether she had been successful. Everything appeared clear, but as the aircraft gained speed for its takeoff, he saw Gina coming back toward them on the dirt next to the landing strip. She stopped, jumped out of her truck, and began to gesture, pointing at the aircraft as it roared past her and lifted off.

Richard waved back, although she couldn't see him through the small window of the DC3. "Yeah, yeah, don't worry," he murmured, "I'll take the lizard back to its habitat." He gave her the finger and whispered, "Go to hell Gina."

The four-hour flight went faster than he expected. Richard had dozed for almost two hours and rehearsed the speech he planned to give at the environmental conference in Guatemala City. They were not far from landing in Mazatlan, in the Mexican state of Sinaloa, when he got up to pee.

When he emerged from the small, cramped toilet right behind the cockpit of the DC3, he marveled again at the mass of cages, equipment and supplies packed into the aircraft. Without this charter, he couldn't imagine how he could have transported everything he needed to Guatemala. Richard felt the plane beginning its descent and returned to his seat.

Below, through his window, he watched a flock of birds swarm over bits of fish thrown from a sleek sport fishing boat. As the western coastline of Mexico came into view, the deep blue color of the Pacific began to fade to aqua in the shallower water. He saw small, rocky islands and then a large one with the El Faro Lighthouse perched at the west end. As the plane lost altitude, it flew over a miles-long boardwalk that snaked along the shoreline and Richard saw an expanse of pink resort hotels and condominiums with swimming pools on their roofs. The white sand and palm trees reminded him of Miami and of Gina. He wondered again, why she had waved so enthusiastically when the plane took off?

They landed minutes later at the Mazatlan International Airport, south of the city, and taxied around to the charter and private air gateway on the far side of the terminal. After four hours in the narrow jump seat, Richard was dying to get out of the confined space of the DC3. While the pilots were assembling their passports, credentials, and the aircraft's documentation, he walked back into the cabin and opened the cargo door. Richard jumped down on the tarmac, stretched, and inhaled the warm humid ocean air. When the pilots emerged, they headed to customs to present their papers and arrange for refueling.

Jorge had endured four hours jammed in amidst all the gear in the aircraft, but he didn't care, because he was curled up next to the Lizard King's cage. If it had been possible, he would have crawled inside, to be even closer to his friend. As it was, he had opened the gate and throughout the flight, had kept his hand on the lizard's back. In addition to feeling the warm and wonderful sensation that emanated from the Lizard's bony skin, Jorge had felt a new feeling, a sense of optimism and well-being that he hadn't experienced since his mother had held him years ago. He thought about his collection of geckos and lizards. Had anyone released them? It didn't matter. Jorge was done with these little creatures; he didn't need them anymore. He had seen the strength and power of the Lizard King and was filled with self-assurance. He was no longer the Cuiza. He was Jorge.

When he felt the jolt as the plane hit the runway, he knew that now it was truly time to say farewell for the last time.

"Chik, chik, chik." *Goodbye again, Lizard King. We are both going home.*

He watched through the open cargo door as the three men walked away from the aircraft. When he could no longer see them, Jorge jumped out of the plane. There was no one in sight, but nearby, several construction trucks were parked next to piles of cinder blocks, bags of cement, and lumber. He ran to the trucks—it was easy to scramble beneath one of the larger ones. It reminded it him of crawling under his mother's bed.

He had no idea how far it was to Culiacán, or how he would get there, but he had heard of Mazatlan and knew his home was nearby. Jorge could take care of himself in Mexico and somehow he would make his way to Culiacán. He remembered what the Lizard King had told him so many times—*todo va bien*—and ran toward the fence behind the terminal building.

Jose Miguel sat in his battered truck and waited for the airplane from America. They were coming from Mazatlan directly to *Aeropuerto de Chiquimula*, a deserted dirt landing strip twenty kilometers from his home in the Motagua River Valley. He saw the first raindrops hit his windshield, ran his finger over the crack, and felt the uneven glass. He had planned to replace it when the *ingeniero* returned from Mexico and paid him the $500 for capturing the lizard, but he had never heard from the *ingeniero*. As the weeks passed, Jose Miguel became angry. As he had feared, he had been cheated. The *ingeniero* wasn't going to pay him, and without the money his son would not have the operation to repair his cleft lip and Jose Miguel could not replace his broken windshield. When his anger finally boiled over, he called the *ingeniero's* home in Guatemala City.

"I want to speak to Alejandro Luna,"

"Who is calling?" a woman asked.

"It is Jose Miguel. I have worked for the *ingeniero*. He owes me money. A lot of money."

"I am his wife," the woman said in a frail voice. "I am sorry he cannot pay you. He is dead."

"Dead?"

"He was killed in Mexico. In a gun battle."

Jose Miguel felt as if someone had punched him in the stomach. He gasped for air. "I am sorry, no one told me," he said, and hung up without saying anything further.

The *ingeniero* was dead? He had worried from the start that capturing the reptile was the wrong thing to do. He had stolen something that belonged to the earth and by doing so, had set loose the lizard's demonic scourge. The very night after the *ingeniero* departed for Mexico, Jose Miguel had begun to have dreams of evil. The lizard had spit poison at him. It had sliced him with its forked tongue. It had sent bolts of lightning from its tail. Now he had learned that the foul reptile had actually brought the curse of death down upon the man who had insisted on capturing it. Jose Miguel wondered what had happened to the lizard. He hoped it too was dead, and prayed that its curse had expired with it.

A few days after learning of the *ingeniero's* death, Jose Miguel was surprised to receive a gift from the grave. *Un gran patrón*—Señor Richard Reed from America—had contacted him, told him that he'd gotten his name from the *ingeniero*, and said he was coming in an airplane to collect lizards, snakes, and plants from all over Guatemala. If Jose Miguel wanted to work, *jefe* Richard would pay him twenty dollars per day, for a month or more. Jose Miguel needed the money and agreed immediately without negotiating, but swore to himself that he would not be talked into capturing another beaded lizard.

He was supposed to meet *jefe* Richard at the airport in Guatemala City, but at the last minute, he had been told to bring his truck to *Aeropuerto de Chiquimula*.

Jose Miguel heard the engines before he spotted the plane. It came in from the west, appearing out of the gray afternoon rainclouds. After dropping down and lowering its wheels, it threw up a spray of water and mud when it hit the dirt runway. Jose Miguel drove after the aircraft and by the time he caught up with it at the far end of the strip, the cargo door had opened and three men had climbed out. Jose Miguel watched one of the pilots and another man, who would be *jefe* Richard, wrestle something out of the aircraft and place it on the ground.

Jose Miguel could not believe what he was seeing. "*Dios mio*," he uttered, crossing himself. He ran to look at the familiar cage before he even greeted *jefe* Richard. Inside was the lizard, looking the same as it did weeks ago when Jose Miguel loaded it into the back of the *ingeniero's* Land Cruiser. Jose Miguel bent down to take a closer look and the lizard hissed, moved its body from side to side, and stared at him with its black, evil eyes. Jose Miguel was certain it recognized him. "So you have returned," Jose Miguel said and fingered the small silver crucifix that hung from his neck.

In the morning, he drove into the arid interior of the Motagua River Valley. Jose Miguel had lived all his life on this parched strip of land, sandwiched between the fertile river plains and dense jungle that ascended into the rainforests of the Sierra de Las Minas. Each year more of the dry land was irrigated—soon it would be completely covered with fruit and tobacco plantations. After remaining untouched for thousands of years, the Motagua River Valley was changing quickly, and Jose Miguel wondered how long the lizard would survive.

He headed out on a dirt road and when it vanished, continued across the open land. When he had captured the lizard, it was the end of the dry season. White clouds had filled the hot, blue sky, and the cacti were blooming with yellow and purple flowers. Now the wet season had settled in, the sky was gray and overcast, and the clouds were full of rain. Jose Miguel remembered exactly where he had found the cursed creature. It was near the spot where a huge *Cabeja de Viejo*—an old man cactus—had somehow managed to take root and flourish, long before Jose Miguel was born. He saw it from a distance, and it somehow reassured him that things were still the same, that perhaps life in the river valley had not completely changed. The cactus was huge, it columnar clusters of stems reaching as high as ten meters. Long white hairs covered most of the stems, hiding the black spines underneath. As he approached, a turkey vulture took flight from its perch atop the cactus. Even from inside his truck, Jose Miguel could hear the flapping of the bird's enormous brown wings.

Jose Miguel stopped, possibly in the exact spot where he had parked the day he had captured the reptile. He threw back the tarp and lowered the heavy cage to the ground. Inside, the lizard was pressed up against the gate, pushing against it as if eager to escape. Jose Miguel released the latch, opened the cage, and stepped back. "*Adiós, demonio.* Before God, I'm sorry I ever touched you," he said, and watched the lizard crawl from the cage and start across the hard dirt of the valley floor.

When the Lizard King left the cage, he moved slowly and deliberately over the ground. His forked tongue recognized familiar scent cues.

He was home.

ACKNOWLEDGMENTS

My sincere thanks to the following people, who were so generous with their time and expertise:

Dr. David Kronemeyer, Ph. D. Clinical Psychology, who helped me to imagine Jorge/the Cuiza.

Miguel Estrada, a Guatemalan language expert.

The men at Los Angeles County Fire Department Station 55, who helped me understand the logistics of fighting a fire on Catalina Island.

Dr. Daniel D. Beck, Ph. D. Ecology & Evolutionary Biology, and author of *Biology of Gila Monsters and Beaded Lizards*, who provided invaluable information about these fascinating reptiles.

The Special Agents in the Los Angeles field division of the Drug Enforcement Administration, who advised me on many aspects of DEA operations.

Last, but certainly not least, *Hunahpú*, the Mayan maize god, who took time from his busy schedule to visit me in my dreams, teach me his ancient language, and allow me to watch a ritual sacrifice.

Motagua Valley Beaded Lizard picture from Daniel Ariano, Universidad del Valle de Guatemala.

ABOUT THE AUTHOR

 alibu, California resident Kurt Kamm
has written a series of firefighter mystery
novels that have won several literary awards.
His newest novel, *The Lizard's Tale*, provides a
unique look inside the activities of the Mexican
drug cartels and the men dedicated to stopping
them. Kurt has used his contact with CalFire, Los
Angeles County and Ventura County Fire Departments, as well as the
ATF and DEA to write fact-based ("faction") novels. He has attended
classes at El Camino Fire Academy and trained in wildland firefighting,
arson investigation and hazardous materials response. He has also
attended the ATF and DEA Citizen's Academies. After graduating from
the DEA Citizen's Academy in 2014, he began work on *The Lizard's Tale*.

Kurt has built an avid fan base among first responders and other
readers. A graduate of Brown University and Columbia Law School,
Kurt was previously a financial executive and semi-professional bicycle
racer. He was also Chairman of the UCLA/Jonsson Comprehensive
Cancer Center Foundation for several years.

Visit Kurt Kamm's website at **KurtKamm.com**

ALSO BY KURT KAMM

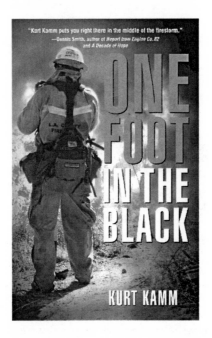

ONE FOOT IN THE BLACK – A Wildland Firefighter's Story

"Kurt Kamm has been there with the firefighters, step by step,
and you will feel in the pages of this book that you are right there
in the middle of a firestorm as well."

—DENNIS SMITH, author of *Report From Engine Co. 82* and *A Decade of Hope*

"With *One Foot in the Black*, Kurt Kamm has used the tools of popular
fiction to shine a light on the inner workings of the wildland fire service.
The tortured main character, who tries to pull a brutalized life together
by joining Cal Fire, the Golden State's fire protection agency, takes us
on a journey from training ground to fire ground that vividly captures
the sense of family, of pulling together, of physical challenge and
mortal danger that go with this increasingly vital occupation."

—JOHN N. MACLEAN, author of *Fire on the Mountain* and other fire books.

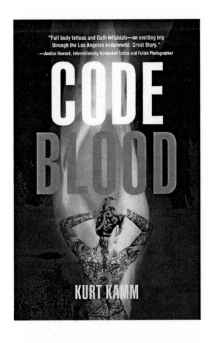

CODE BLOOD

An edgy L.A. Noir thriller! Kamm takes the reader into the world of emergency medicine, the science of stem cell research, and the unsettling world of blood fetishism and body parts.

Code Blood won three FIRST PLACE national literary competitions:
2012 International Book Awards, Fiction: Cross Genre category
National Indie Excellent Book Awards® – Faction (fiction based on fact)
The 2012 USA Best Book Awards Fiction: Horror

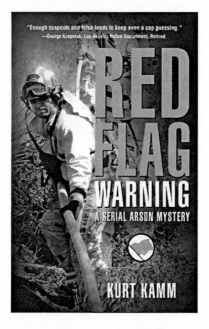

RED FLAG WARNING – A Serial Arson Mystery

A serial arsonist tries to burn down Malibu.
Can the Arson Squad stop the fires?

"NiteHeat is memorable—another lunatic out setting fires."
—MIKE COLE, CalFire Battalion Chief, Law Enforcement

Red Flag Warning won two FIRST PLACE
national mystery competitions:
The Written Art Awards – Mystery/Thriller 2010
Royal Dragonfly – Mystery Category 2011

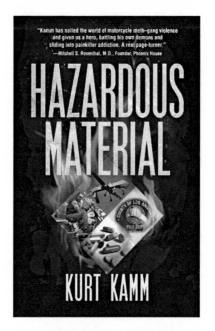

HAZARDOUS MATERIAL

A firefighter battles painkiller addiction and
the Vagos outlaw motorcycle gang.

Hazardous Material won several literary awards:
Best Novel 2013 – Public Safety Writers Association
2012 Hackney Literary Award for best novel of the year
Reader's Favorite 2013 – Finalist – Urban Fiction

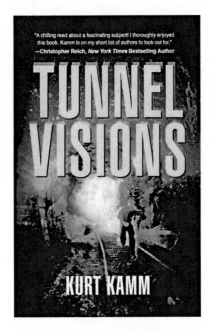

TUNNEL VISIONS

As California faces its driest year in history, terrorists threaten
the Los Angeles water supply.

"A chilling read about a fascinating subject.
I thoroughly enjoyed this book."
—CHRISTOPHER REICH, *New York Times* bestselling author.

Tunnel Visions was a finalist in the 2014 USA Best Book Awards.